Sail to my heart

Rachel Dyer

I would like to thank everyone who has supported me throughout the years with my books. Everyone's encouragement, and critique, has helped me spread my wings and really explore the world of writing.

My biggest, most generous thanks go out to:

Sarah Secules

You've always been there for me throughout my writing adventures and I love you for always pushing me to go beyond my comfort zone. Thank you for always believing in me!

I also want to include a few others who have been there for me:

Stephanie Brown
Annette Thomas
&
Steven Dyer

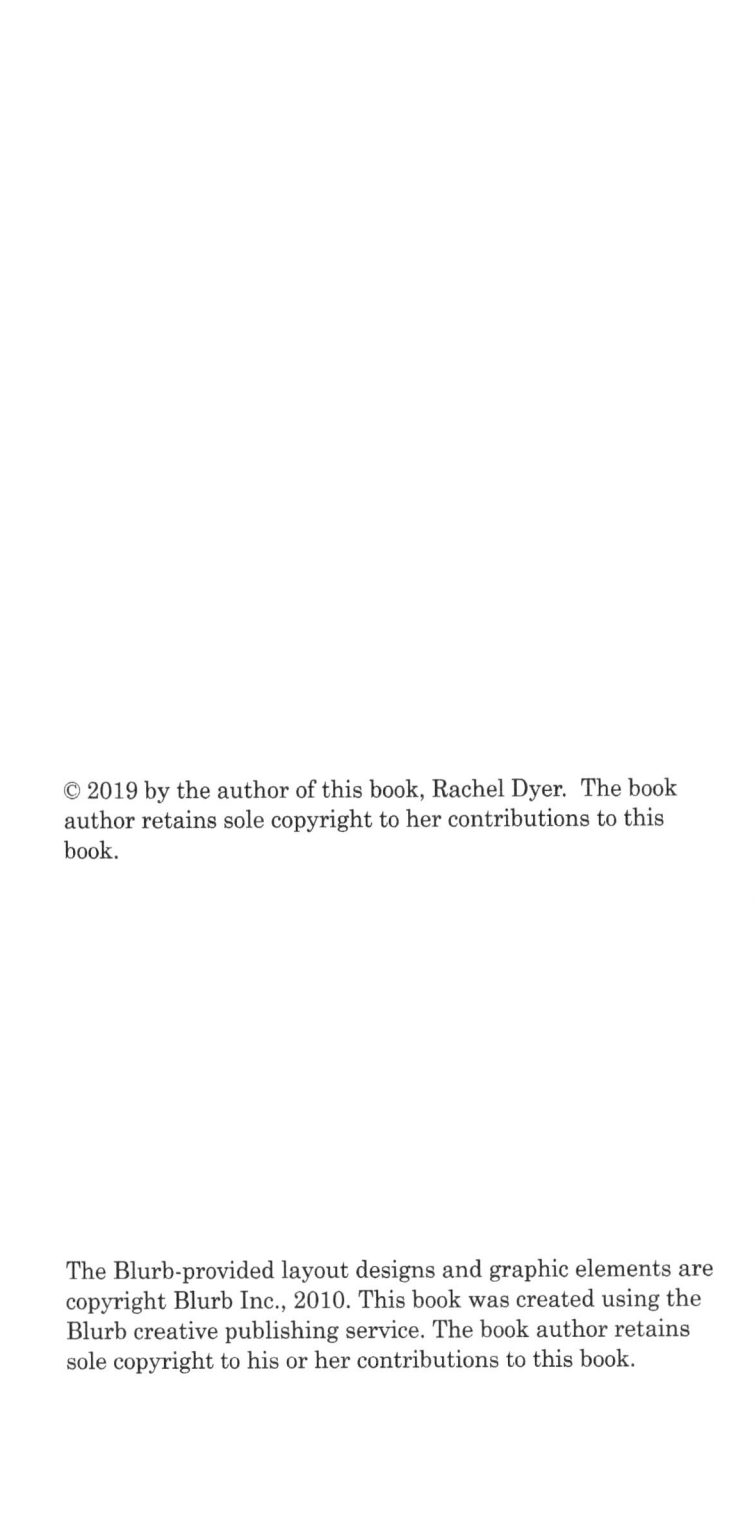

© 2019 by the author of this book, Rachel Dyer. The book author retains sole copyright to her contributions to this book.

The Blurb-provided layout designs and graphic elements are copyright Blurb Inc., 2010. This book was created using the Blurb creative publishing service. The book author retains sole copyright to his or her contributions to this book.

December 21st, 2018

"Good morning! This is your captain speaking. We are beginning our descent into New York City. Please fasten your seat belts, put your tray tables up, and make sure your seats are in their upright position."

Twenty-seven year old Hannah Lane secured her tray, and tucked her journal that she had been writing in into her purse.

"Hannah, this is so exciting! Can you believe our cruise vacation is finally here?" exclaimed Kaylee, Hannah's older sister. Sitting next to Kaylee was her husband of eleven years, Aaron.

"Now if we can just find Hunter at the airport, we will be all set," commented Aaron, checking his cell phone. Kaylee reprimanded him for having his phone out before the plane landed. Aaron only rolled his eyes.

Hannah gazed out the small airplane window at the snowy New York City scenery coming into view. She had almost forgotten about the fourth addition to their party.

Hunter McFarland. Hannah had not seen, or thought of him since Kaylee's wedding so many years back. Hunter had been Aaron's best man and Hannah had been Kaylee's maid of honor. She remembered him being really attractive and very funny. At the time, she had developed somewhat of a crush on him, but he didn't seem to really notice her. A fluttery feeling swelled in her stomach at the thought of seeing his handsome face again.

As the airplane pulled into their designated gate, the passengers hastily made their exit. Hannah grabbed her backpack and jacket and followed Kaylee and Aaron as they made their way off of the plane.

The airport had Christmas decorations glittering throughout each gate. Christmas lights were wrapped around each flight desk and some of the staff wore Santa hats. Hannah smiled at the holiday cheer. Christmas was her favorite time of year. It was going to be interesting spending the winter holiday in the Caribbean.

As the group reached the airport lobby, Hannah excused herself to use the restroom. After washing her hands, she took a good look in the mirror. Her bright, curly red hair flowed over her shoulders to her waist. The curls were a little unruly at the moment, but there was no time to waste on preening her locks. Taking a deep breath, Hannah took one final glance at the full length mirror.

"Guess this will have to do," she said to her reflection. Pushing her hair out of her face, Hannah went to rejoin her group. She looked around the lobby to see if she could spot her sister. It was never hard to spot a Lane. Each had brilliant red hair that could be spotted easily in a crowd.

The luck of the Irish, she giggled to herself.

Hannah's eyes continued to roam around the room.

"Ah ha! There they are," she voiced, making her way to what seemed to be three people instead of two. Hannah recognized the face standing behind Aaron.

Hunter.

~~*~*~*

Hunter McFarland had been in the airport lobby waiting for his long time friend to land with his wife and her sister. He had been friends with Aaron since grade school, but after high school Hunter went to New York for business school. He had kept in touch with Aaron and had flown back to their home town of Charlotte, North Carolina to be in Aaron's wedding.

Hunter smirked thinking of Kaylee's sister, Hannah. He had walked her up and down the aisle as duty required. She was a sweet girl with fiery red just like Kaylee, and she was cute. He could tell that she was interested in him, but she seemed too young to get involved with.

Hunter shook his head. It's not like he could have dated her even if she was older. He didn't know anything about Hannah. They didn't even live in the same state.

I had a career to think about anyway, he thought to himself.

"Hunter! Over here!" shouted a male voice, bringing Hunter out of his reverie. He looked around to locate the voice he knew was Aaron's, but spotted Kaylee's red hair first. Hunter stood and met the couple as they walked toward him.

"Man, it's good to see you!" said Aaron, pulling Hunter into a bear hug.

"I know. It's been too long," Hunter agreed smiling.

"Hopefully that length of time didn't make you forget me," joked Kaylee.

"Who could forget this hair!?" he replied, grasping a wisp of her hair between his fingers.

"It's always the hair," she rolled her eyes playfully, returning her hair to its previous state of rest.

"How is the real estate business treating you these days?" asked Aaron, shifting his carry-on bag from one shoulder to the other.

"Honestly, I can't complain. Luxury real estate has its highs and lows, but when it's high it's boomin'," Hunter answered, displaying a wide smile. He loved his job.

Before Aaron could get his next statement out, a flash of red came jogging up behind them. Hannah stopped beside her sister, her curls still quivering from her sudden stop.

"Hey, guys! I'm sorry I kept you waiting," she said, letting out a breath.

Hunter stood in awe of what he was seeing. Gone was the skinny girl he had walked with at the wedding eleven years ago. Before him stood a beautiful woman whose green eyes seemed to pierce his very soul. Hunter remembered her eyes being captivating, but her new physique left him spellbound. And the freckles around her cheeks, jaw, and pert nose were the icing on the cake. It was like she had magically transformed.

An awkward moment passed by before Hunter could come to his senses. Snapping back to the current, he stuck out his hand to greet her.

"It's Hannah, right?" he asked, trying to play it cool. No need for her to think he was some weird creep staring at her. Hannah smiled, showing a perfect set of white teeth.

"That's me. Nice to see you again, Hunter," she replied, shaking his outstretched hand. Her soft skin sent tingles up his spine.

Well, I can see this is going to be an interesting cruise, thought Hunter as the group made their way to baggage claim.

~~*~*~*

The taxi ride over to the pier was somewhat of a blur to Hannah. She was surprised that seeing Hunter didn't spark butterflies the way she thought they would upon seeing him again. Yes, he definitely was handsome. More so than she remembered with his strikingly chiseled features. But Hannah couldn't shake the feeling that something was off about him.

The cab pulled up to the pier and all of Hannah's previous thoughts dissipated. There before her was the biggest ship she had ever seen. Her jaw went slack as she stepped out of the taxi van.

"You're going to catch flies," giggled Kaylee, nudging Hannah playfully in the arm as she walked passed.

"Kaylee, this ship is *massive*!" exclaimed Hannah, ignoring her sister's jest. She pulled her jacket closer to her neck as the swift winter wind blew.

Deck after deck flooded Hannah's vision as her eyes roamed higher and higher. One deck was completely committed to lifeboats that swung alongside the deck. She had a hard time taking it all in as they walked closer to the huge vessel.

The cruise terminal was very busy. People were going every which way and it seemed like there was no organization at all. It was even busier than the airport had been. Hannah stayed close to her group and followed them to the security line. They passed through an x-ray scanner similar to the one at the airport. After passing through security, Hannah safely placed her passport and cruise documents into her backpack.

Next came the check in lines. The large room held many lines sectioned off by long, black dividers. Some lines were much shorter than the one Hannah's group had gone in, but she realized that those lines were for the handicapped.

Hannah's mind was so overwhelmed that she stopped a few yards back from the line her group had already entered. She looked around the large room and through the windows where she could catch glimpses of the ever growing cruise ship. She wasn't paying attention as a small group of young men came barreling through the room for the check in lines.

Before Hannah had time to register what was happening, she found herself being flung through the air. Her backpack landed a few feet away from her before she herself landed on the hard tile. She felt the breath rush out of her as her chest heaved to take in air. Hannah heard someone jogging briskly toward her and felt a strong hand on her shoulder.

"Hannah, are you okay?" asked a deep voice. Hannah looked up to see Hunter kneeling beside her. His large blue eyes looked down at her with concern.

Finally, she was able to get her lungs to work. Air came flooding in and Hannah became more aware of her surroundings. She realized she had had the wind knocked out of her.

Immediately, she looked around to locate her backpack. Upon finding it, she saw her papers had been scattered across the floor.

"Oh, no...I need to make sure I'm not missing anything," she sighed, preparing to stand. As she put pressure on her left hand, a small cry of pain escaped her lips as she fell back down.

"Whoa there. Let me help you up," Hunter instructed, lightly tugging her elbow and pulling her up effortlessly. Hannah moved her wrist around and felt a sharp, stabbing pain with each movement.

No! This isn't happening! I can NOT have a broken wrist on this cruise! Hannah screamed inwardly.

~~*~*~*

Hunter noticed Hannah wince as she tried to move her wrist around. Small tears formed at the corner of her eyes and she bit her lip to hold in another whimper of pain. Instantly Hunter felt the need to hold her in his arms. He was surprised at the intensity of his emotions.

"Hannah, is everything alright?" asked Kaylee entering the scene.

"Yeah, I'm alright. My wrist hurts, though, and my papers are tossed all over the floor," Hannah answered, pointing to where her purse had landed.

"Here, I'll help you with that," Kaylee offered as she guided her sister over to collect her things.

Hunter looked around the room for the group of guys that had run into Hannah. Spotting them standing in one of the lines waiting to check in, Hunter walked over with anger in his eyes. They didn't even seem phased at what they had just done.

"Hey! You guys need to watch where you're going. You don't seem to realize that you knocked a woman to the floor while you were bull rushing to the line," chided Hunter firmly.

"Hey, man, *she's* the one lollygagging in the middle of the room," replied one of the guys as he shrugged his shoulders.

Hunter became furious at the his callous response. He grabbed the lanky man by his jacket and jerked him forward.

"You listen to me! I oughta..." Hunter threatened with bravado before seeing Aaron step in between him and the target of his rage.

"Hunter, no! Just let him go," urged Aaron, nudging Hunter away from the object of his rage. He released his grip on the stranger and allowed Aaron to usher him back to the line where Kaylee and Hannah were now standing.

Hunter gazed down at Hannah's wrist. She was holding it tenderly in her right hand. He hoped it wasn't broken.

~~*~*~*

After making it through the check in process, they started boarding. As Hannah walked up the gangway to the ship, the frustration of her accident started to fester in her mind. At the end of the gangway there was a crew member checking the passengers' cruise tickets.

"Boarding tickets, please," requested the female crew member. Hannah fumbled to open her backpack and winced as the pain flared in her wrist. Finally, she was able to pull out her ticket.

"Ma'am, we have first aid available if you

need someone to look at your hand," the polite crew member offered. Hannah hadn't even thought about that possibility.

"Actually, yes, that would be very helpful. Can you tell me how to get there?" she asked.

The crew member smiled and handed Hannah a map of the ship, pointing to where she needed to go. Hannah thanked her and met up with her group that had entered the warm main atrium.

Hannah was taken aback by the beauty of the large room. Looking up, it felt like she could see for miles. She could see every deck and at the top there was a huge glass window that allowed bright light in from the sun.

Christmas decorations were literally everywhere. A gigantic Christmas tree was in the middle of the atrium glittering with lights and decorations. Garland wrapped with lights wound around every railing you could see. The elevators going up and down from floor to floor had red and green lights glowing from underneath. Christmas had exploded on this ship and she couldn't have been more in awe.

"Hannah, we were thinking we would find our cabins and then get a bite to eat," Kaylee stated, pulling Hannah out of her euphoric state of mind.

"Well, I was wondering if maybe you would come with me to the medical facility so I could get my wrist checked out?" Hannah asked curiously. Kaylee nodded her head.

"Hey, guys, I'm going to go with Hannah to get her wrist looked at. Why don't you get your stuff set up in the cabins and we'll meet you there," she instructed.

"Okay. Our bags probably won't be there until later on tonight. Why don't we look at the map and check out the places to eat? We'll be here in the atrium waiting for you," said Aaron.

"That sounds good. See you soon," Haylee smiled, giving her husband a sweet kiss.

At the medical facility the doctor took a look at Hannah's wrist. She wasn't too fond of the twisting and turning of her wrist while being examined.

"Okay, well, I can say it's not broken, but it is sprained. The good news is you wont need a splint, but you will need to keep it wrapped for a few days. After that you will only need to wrap it if it starts to hurt or swell. You can take Tylenol for the pain," instructed the doctor as he completed his figure eight wrap on her wrist.

"Thank you for seeing me," Hannah smiled, shaking the doctor's hand.

Later on that evening, Hannah relaxed on her bed. Her bags had been delivered to her cabin and she was able to get her stuff situated in the closet and dressers. With all the excitement of the day, Hannah found herself exhausted. Pulling out her journal, she decided she would document the events of the day.

December 22nd, 2018

Hannah's fears came to life the next day. Her wrist was very sore and she could hardly move it. The doctor had said for the first few days it could be this way, but she was hoping he would have been wrong. She showered and even *that* proved to be difficult. Once she was dressed in her jeans and green long sleeve shirt, she went out to the hallway to meet the rest of her party.

"Hey, Hannah! How's the wrist?" asked Aaron as he shut the door to the cabin he shared with Kaylee.

"Not all that great," frowned Hannah, looking down at her tightly re wrapped wrist. She wasn't sure she had wrapped it quite as well as the doctor had.

"Aww, Hannah, I'm sorry. So that means

you probably shouldn't go swimming today," Kaylee sighed as her shoulders drooped.

Is it even warm enough to swim yet? Hannah questioned inwardly.

"If you guys planned on swimming today that's okay if I don't go. I can do something else during that time. Besides, I need to take it easy if I want this thing to heal," she said, pointing to her wrist.

At that moment, Hunter came out of his cabin to join the group. He had a bag over his shoulder with a bathing suit peaking out. He walked over to Hannah looking down at her wrist.

"How is your wrist feeling today?" he asked, lightly bringing her arm closer to him.

"It's pretty sore. I'm going to skip out on the swimming," she answered, slipping her arm out of his hand. His touch gave her shivers and she couldn't tell if it was a good or bad feeling.

"I can stay with you if you'd like some company," offered Hunter, his expression innocent. Hannah thought about his offer for a moment. Did she want to hang out with Hunter alone? It was harmless enough, but something kept her from agreeing.

"No, that's okay. Don't stop your plans for me. I'll have plenty of time to go swimming," she answered, waving her hand to shoo off the idea. Hunter frowned, but didn't push it.

"Do you want to meet up for lunch?" asked Kaylee.

"Yeah, that sounds fine. I'll meet you in the atrium around noon?" Hannah suggested. Everyone nodded in agreement and went their separate ways.

After having a light breakfast, Hannah took the elevator to deck five. She walked by an art gallery, casino, a candy store and a few jewelry shops before deciding she wanted to walk the promenade on deck nine.

Once outside, the cool sea breeze blew her hair all about. She smiled and inhaled the alluring scent. The sky was a beautiful blue and the sun's rays felt good on her freckled cheeks.

Looking to the left and right, the deck seemed to go on forever. There were deck chairs as far as the eye could see. Hannah couldn't resist the pull of the ocean view. She walked over to the rail and watched as the water swept past her in large, rolling waves far below.

I could stay in this spot for the rest of my life, thought Hannah, sighing contently.

But after a while she shivered and decided she should walk around to keep warm. How her group could swim in this cold was beyond her. When she reached the stern of the ship, she decided to take a break on one of the deck chairs.

Hannah's wrist was starting to bother her. She looked down at the wrapping job she had done earlier and decided it needed to be adjusted. Pulling up her sleeve, she unwound the elastic bandage. She could feel the blood creeping into her hand.

Maybe I wrapped it too tight, she thought, as she flexed her fingers.

She knew she wasn't supposed to exercise her wrist until the pain subsided, but Hannah moved her wrist slightly from side to side. Instantly there was twinge of pain and she felt stupid for even attempting the exercise. She didn't want to be patient, but it didn't look like she had a choice.

Now to redo this wrap, she sighed inwardly, trying to remember how the doctor had wrapped it. Hannah tried to get a solid grip started, but it kept slipping out when she would go to wind it higher. Frustrated, Hannah tried again. A third time, a fourth time and still she could not get it to stay wrapped.

"Do you mind if I help?" asked a soft male voice next to her.

Hannah jumped in surprise at the sudden, unexpected company. Her first thought was embarrassment at the thought of someone seeing her fail at doing a simple wrist wrap. Her cheeks flamed red as she turned to face the kind man who offered his help. Hannah gasped as she looked up into the most mesmerizing blue-green eyes.

~~*~*~*

Chace Devons had been lounging on a deck chair soaking up some sun when he noticed a flicker of red in his peripheral. Glancing over, he saw a petite redheaded woman sitting on a deck chair not too far from where he was. He watched her inconspicuously as she unraveled a medical bandage from her wrist. She winced in pain as she tried to move it and Chace found himself wincing with her. He knew what it felt like to have a broken wrist.

The red haired beauty started to wrap

her hand back up, but he noticed she was having trouble securing it. He watched as her attempts failed numerous times before deciding to see if she would let him help.

Chace walked over to her and asked if she would mind if he helped. He saw her jump at his quiet arrival.

"Sorry, I didn't mean to scare you," said Chace, backing up. When she turned to face him, his heart skipped a beat. Her face was unlike any he had ever seen. The way her hair framed her face, covered in a smattering of small freckles, was stunning. But most striking were her eyes. Deep green emeralds peered up at him innocently.

Shaking his head, Chace sat down on the deck chair next to her. An impish smile turned her pink lips up. Could someone really be this beautiful?

"I'm sure you can probably do a better job than me," she laughed grimacing.

"Well, it does help when you have two free hands," Chace responded, raising his hands up to his chest and wiggling his fingers. That earned him a laugh from the beauty. He smiled and extended his hand.

"I'm Chace," he said, introducing himself.

"Hannah," she responded, slipping her good hand into his and shaking it. He felt a warm shiver when their hands made contact and their eyes met again.

This girl could be trouble with those eyes, Chace thought, slowly pulling his hand out of hers.

"Well, Hannah, let's get that wrist

wrapped up," stated Chace reaching, for her bandage. Hannah offered her left arm over to him and he carefully began to wrap her wrist. He looked up once to see her biting her lip as he got closer to her injury. He made sure to be extra careful around it, but also making sure to get it firm and secure.

"There we go," Chace announced, letting go of her slender arm. She looked at her newly bandaged hand and smiled in approval.

"I really appreciate it. There was no way I would have been able to do that with just one hand," said Hannah, raising her good hand to her chest and wiggling her fingers like he had moments earlier. Chace chuckled, running his fingers through his hair.

"I'm glad I could help. If you don't mind me asking, what happened? The way you were cringing makes me think this is somewhat fresh," Chace commented, shifting to get more comfortable on the deck chair.

"Yeah, this happened not even twenty-four hours ago. My sister, brother-in-law and his friend are here with me. They were waiting in line to get checked in at the cruise terminal. I was a little slower. I couldn't help taking everything in," she grinned blushing.

"So anyway, there were some guys that came barging through the terminal and they mulled in to me. I flew sideways and landed on my wrist. I didn't figure that out until after I got the wind knocked out of me," said Hannah, rolling her eyes and shaking her head.

Chace's eyes went wide as he listened. He felt sorry for her. Who wants to be hurt before going on a cruise?

"That's awful. Did the guys say anything to you? An apology or something?" he questioned. Hannah shook her head no, shrugging her shoulders.

"No, nothing. My brother-in-law's friend, Hunter, said something, though. I thought he was going to start a fight," she answered.

Chace thought it was interesting that out of all the people she mentioned were with her, Hunter was the only name she revealed.

Maybe he's more than a friend, he thought. For some reason that didn't sit well with him and that confused him.

I just met this girl and all of the sudden I have feelings of jealousy for some guy she mentions? Get a hold of yourself, Chace! he thought, chastising himself.

"Sounds like you have a protector," Chace mentioned, looking at Hannah for any clue of her feelings toward this guy. He felt ridiculous for even saying that, but male curiosity won over anything else at that moment.

"I don't know about that. I barely know him. He was my brother-in-law, Aaron's, best man when Aaron married my sister, Kaylee, eleven years ago. I've only seen him a handful of times. I don't know why he acted so brash," Hannah answered, almost like she was talking to herself.

Chace sighed with relief at her answer. He couldn't understand why, but he felt better talking to her knowing she possibly wasn't attached. He decided to change the direction of their conversation.

"So have you ever been on a cruise before?" he asked, looking around the deck.

"No, this is my first. I've never even been out of the country," Hannah laughed, resting her injured hand up by her chest.

"It's my second, but I've never been to the Caribbean before. My first cruise was to Alaska," said Chace.

"Oh, wow! I bet that was something," she exclaimed, her eyes lighting up.

"It was awesome. Cold, but still it was really fun," he stated.

They sat there in silence for a few moments. Chace wanted to know more about her. Then he got an idea.

"Have you made it around the whole deck yet?"

~~*~*~*

Hannah walked with Chace around the promenade deck for a long time. She enjoyed talking to him and was surprised to see they had made it around to the stern for the second time.

"Hannah!" someone shouted. Looking around, Hannah spotted Hunter coming toward her and Chace. She had forgotten all about meeting up with everyone for lunch.

"We've been waiting for you in the atrium for over a half an hour. Kaylee was getting worried so I told her I'd look for you. Good thing your sister knows you so well. She suggested that you'd be up here walking around," exclaimed Hunter, giving a disapproving look at Chace. Hannah was surprised at the bitterness of his tone. Yes, she was late, but what she was doing was none of his business to judge.

She saw Chace shift from foot to foot beside her and remembered her manners.

"Hunter, this is Chace. Chace this is Hunter," she announced, introducing the two. Chace extended his hand to shake Hunter's. Hunter looked at Chace's hand for a few moments before shaking it briefly.

"Hunter, can you please tell Kaylee and Aaron that I'll meet you guys by the elevators in the atrium in a moment?" Hannah asked. Hunter turned to her, his eyebrows going up. Suddenly, his face became stoic as he turned to leave.

"Yeah, I'll let them know," he said, looking from Hannah to Chace in confusion.

Once Hunter turned the corner, Hannah found herself releasing a pent up breath she didn't realize she had been holding in.

"Well, it sounds like you are wanted elsewhere," said Chace, rubbing the back of his neck with his arm in the air. Hannah saw the muscles in his arms as he reached for his neck. She felt herself shiver, and not because of the slight chill in the air.

"I'm sorry for that awkward encounter. It is my fault. I did forget about telling them that I'd meet up with them for lunch around noon," said Hannah, checking the time on her cell phone.

"Well, I had a really great time talking with you, Hannah," he said, offering a half smile.

Hannah's heart twinged. All of the sudden, lunch didn't sound that appealing. To be honest with herself, she would have loved to walk another round on the deck with Chace.

"Well, what are you doing after dinner? Maybe we can meet up and continue our conversation?" she blurted.

I'm crazy! I have to be! I barely met this man and I'm asking if he wants to meet up later?! How desperate I must seem, thought Hannah, mentally slapping herself.

"Actually, yeah, I would like to meet up with you after dinner. If you don't have anything going on, that is," said Chace, nodding his head to where Hunter had just walked off. Hannah pursed her lips as a smile formed.

"Okay, I'd like that. When and where?" she asked, already getting excited for their next meet up.

"How about around eight-thirty at the stern?" he suggested. Hannah smiled.

"Perfect."

"Great! I'll see you then, Hannah," he said, catching her eyes with his. Her name sounded so good rolling off of his lips. She felt a shiver of excitement course through her body.

"Til then, Chace," she replied.

Turning to leave, she glanced back once more. Chace hadn't moved. His award winning smile was breathtaking.

Slow down, Hannah! Don't get too caught up, her inner voice warned her.

~~*~*~*

After lunch, Aaron and Hunter wanted to check out the game room/arcade. They asked the girls if they wanted to join them, but they declined. Instead, Kaylee and Hannah went to one of the many lounges on board. Once she was seated at the bar, Hannah looked over the drink menu.

"I would love a mojito right about now," said Kaylee, looking over the available selections.

"You and your mojitos," laughed Hannah.

"What can I say? They are good!" Kaylee declared.

Hannah decided on a sweet martini. As the two waited for their drinks, Hannah gazed around at the lounge. Christmas decor was strung throughout the bar. Small Christmas trees were on each end of the bar and red rope lights illuminated a pathway around the room.

"So, Hunter told us that you were late because of some guy you were talking to?" Kaylee questioned, turning her bar stool to face Hannah. Hannah blushed slightly and pursed her lips in a smile.

"His name is Chace," she replied. She went on to tell her sister about the gorgeous guy she had spent the morning walking and talking with.

"You're meeting up with him tonight?!" asked Kaylee, clearly shocked. Hannah took a sip of her martini.

"I know, it's crazy, isn't it? I don't know, Kaylee. There's just something about him. He's sweet, funny and really easy to talk to. I probably would have been even later getting to lunch with you guys if Hunter hadn't found me," she admitted sheepishly.

"Speaking of Hunter, what happened when he found you? When he got back to us he seemed kind of upset," Kaylee mentioned, finishing her mojito.

"Nothing happened. He came off as kind of rude when he said you guys had been waiting," Hannah recalled, still bothered by his reaction on the promenade deck.

"I wonder what got him all bent out of shape," Kaylee pondered.

"Beats me. He was rude toward Chace, too. Chace reached out to shake his hand after I introduced them, and Hunter seemed reluctant to shake his hand back. I don't understand why," sighed Hannah, sliding off of her bar stool.

The two walked out onto the deck and over to the railing. There were big white, puffy clouds in the sky, but the sun still shone brightly overhead warming their exposed skin.

"What if it was Chace? Kaylee suggested. Hannah turned to her sister bewildered.

"What was?"

"Maybe it was Chace's presence that set off Hunter," Kaylee pointed out.

Why would Chace upset Hunter? He didn't even say anything.

"That doesn't make sense to me," said Hannah, shaking her head.

"Well, what if Hunter *likes* you?" suggested Kaylee, adjusting her hair from the blowing wind.

"*What?!*" Hannah chocked out. Kaylee rolled her eyes.

"Seriously, Hannah? Think about it. At the cruise terminal, when you got hurt, who rushed to your aid? Who goes to defend you when facing those college boys that ran into you? Who offered to stay with you this morning while Aaron and I went swimming?" Kaylee pointed out, counting off each question with her fingers.

Hannah pushed herself off the railing and started to pace between two deck chairs.

This is stupid. Hunter doesn't know me from Eve. He certainly paid no attention to me several years ago at Kaylee's wedding, and I'm pretty sure it was painfully obvious that I was attracted to him. I mean, yes, he helped me in the terminal. Yes, he offered to hang out with me since I couldn't go swimming. He could have just been being nice.

All these thoughts swirled around in her head as she paced back and forth. Finally, Kaylee interrupted her inner turmoil.

"Hannah, you're going to wear a hole in the deck," she stated, stepping in front of Hannah's path. Hannah stopped inches from her sister, her hair whooshing to over her face. Brushing it her back with her fingers, Hannah looked at her sister.

"Kaylee, I think you're mistaken. He's probably just being nice."

"Hannah, you're so naive," laughed Kaylee, heading back toward the lounge. Hannah followed disagreeing.

"You just watch. I'll prove my theory. Let's go find the guys. I'm going to ask Aaron if he'd like to explore a deck with me. You say that you want to go back to your room for a bit. I bet you ten bucks Hunter will offer to take you," Kaylee smiled, squinting her eyes at Hannah.

Hannah rolled her eyes at her sister.

"You're crazy," she laughed.

Hannah and Kaylee found Aaron and Hunter at the arcade playing a racing game.

"Come on, baby, come on!" Hunter chanted to himself.

"No way, man. *I'm* going to win this one!" Aaron claimed, gritting through his teeth. Hannah stood behind them and saw that they were neck and neck on the last lap of a race. Kaylee mouthed the word "men" to Hannah, making her giggle.

"NO!" Hunter shouted, releasing the steering wheel of the game. His shout made Hannah jump.

"Finally!" declared Aaron thrusting his fists up in victory.

"Next time you won't be so lucky," Hunter threatened light-heartedly.

"Okay, *boys*, do you think you can tear yourselves away from the games for now?" asked Kaylee, playfully shoving Aaron's head. He caught her hand and kissed, it winking at her. Hannah looked away and happened to glance over at Hunter. He was looking at her with a small smile on his face, making Hannah blush.

"Aaron, I was wondering if you would like to explore one of the decks with me?" asked

Kaylee, just as she said she would. Aaron shrugged his shoulders.

"Sure, that'd be fine," he replied.

Kaylee looked over at Hannah, cueing her for the next part of their bet.

Oh yeah...

"I think I'm going to go back to my cabin for a while," said Hannah, delivering her line.

"I can walk back with you. I'll be heading that way, too," Hunter offered.

It took all of Hannah's control not to let her eyes bulge. Haylee had been right on point. She snuck a peek at her sister. Kaylee wore the smile of the Cheshire cat.

Unbelievable! Hannah's mind shouted. Kaylee looked at her nodding her head, prompting her to accept Hunter's offer.

"Yeah, that would be fine," Hannah agreed, offering him a smile. His return smile was dazzling.

He's just being friendly, she reminded herself. *Isn't he?*

~~*~*~*

Hunter walked toward the elevator with Hannah. He was grateful for some time alone with her. Wanting to talk to her ever since he had seen her with that other guy had been all he thought about. But Hannah seemed quiet.

"How is your wrist feeling?" he asked, looking down at her hand. He noticed it was wrapped differently than that morning.

"It's not too bad. Chace adjusted the bandage for me. I guess I'm no good at wrapping it myself with a bum hand," she chuckled. Hunter tried to conceal his look of annoyance at the mention of that guy.

As the doors to the elevator opened, he put is hand on the small of her back and walked into the elevator with her beside him. Hannah took a step forward to push the button for their cabin deck. He contemplated placing his hand on her back again, but thought he might be pushing it.

Hunter couldn't lie to himself. He was very attracted to Hannah. He liked her. As she stood beside him staring out the glass elevator, he couldn't help but stare at her beauty. Her lips were slightly parted and she looked like she was concentrating on something. It surprised him how strongly the longing was to kiss her.

The elevator dinged at their deck and the doors parted, revealing the extensive row of cabins. Hunter allowed Hannah to exit first. They turned left and started down the long hallway to their cabins. He wanted to keep her talking before they reached their rooms.

"Hey, look...I'm sorry for the way I acted when I found you earlier," said Hunter apologetically. Hannah looked at the carpeted floor, but said nothing for a moment.

"It's alright, Hunter. I'm just confused about it," she confessed, turning her head to look at him. He couldn't blame her for that. He had acted like a jealous boyfriend. Sighing, he tried to figure out a way to explain without being too blunt.

"I don't know what came over me. Maybe I was just really hungry," said Hunter, throwing out a random excuse.

Stupid, Hunter. Really stupid, he thought, mentally bashing himself. The last thing he wanted to start doing was lying. The first part was true. He really *didn't* know what had come over him.

Hannah stopped walking and he realized that they had reached her cabin.

So much for the long walk, he thought.

"Well, again, I'm sorry for letting my stomach make a fool out of me," he grinned childishly.

"Don't worry about it," said Hannah, shooing away the topic with her hand. He saw her gasp in pain as she held her wrist.

"Are you okay?" he asked, moving closer to her.

"Yeah, I'm alright. I just forget sometimes that this wrist is injured and I shouldn't be waving it around," Hannah answered, sighing.

"I should get in my cabin now. After that stupid move I just made, I think I'm going to ice my wrist," she commented, laughing off her forgetfulness.

"You're not stupid," Hunter corrected, lowering his voice. Hannah stopped laughing and looked up at him. Her eyes seemed full of questions and confusion. Was it possible that she was attracted to him, too? Was she confused about her feelings for him?

Without turning away, she whispered "Thank you" to him with a smile. Hunter lightly swept his fingers down the length of her arm. He could feel her tremble and hoped he wasn't overstepping his boundaries. She stepped back slightly and scanned her cruise card to open her door.

"Thanks for walking me to my cabin," she smiled, waving her good hand as she entered her room.

"Anytime," he smiled.

Hannah nodded and closed the door behind her. Hunter exhaled a big breath and turned toward his own cabin. He still couldn't read how she was responding to his advances. He would have to rely on patience.

~~*~*~*

Hannah heard a knock at her door, sending her bolting out of bed. She had fallen asleep. The sunlight that had once been shining through her window was now fading.

Oh crap! How long was I out for? she thought, reaching for her phone. The time read six o'clock. Another knock resounded.

"Coming!" she called panicking.

"What have you been doing? It's almost time for dinner," said Kaylee, pointing to her watch. Hannah yawned, rubbing her eyes with her fingertips.

"Sorry, Kaylee. I guess I dozed off," she answered. The last thing she remembered was lying on her bed trying to sort out what was going on with Hunter.

"Well, let me in so I can help you get ready. You don't want to go to dinner looking like a ragamuffin," said Kaylee, letting herself in. Hannah shut the door and walked over to the mirror. Her hair was completely out of control.

Kaylee came over and started to brush Hannah's hair. She brushed it the way their mother had when they were kids. Usually, Hannah would have protested to her sister doing her hair like a child, but she welcomed it tonight. By the time Kaylee was done with the rigorous brushing routine, Hannah's hair was smooth and shiny.

"I think you do that better than Mom did," she giggled, running her fingers through her silky hair.

"Well, Mom always said we would have a lifetime of torture with our Irish locks," said Kaylee, primping her own hair in the mirror.

"What are you going to wear tonight?" asked Kaylee, walking toward Hannah's closet.

"No, no. I can pick out my own clothes, thank you," Hannah called out as her sister disappeared behind the closet door. Hannah turned the corner and gave her sister a stern look.

"Okay, okay! I'll get out of your way," surrendered Kaylee, giggling as she backed away with her hands in the air.

"Meet us in the atrium," Kaylee instructed as she left.

When Hannah was alone, she looked through her closet for what dress she wanted to wear. She had gone shopping back home for the cutest casual dresses and a few formal dresses for dinner on the cruise.

Tonight she decided on a light blue, long sleeved casual dress with a moderate V neck.

It hugged her frame from the waist up and then flowed freely down to her mid thigh. She liked that it was dressy, but not overly formal. With the dress she chose gladiator sandals. Hannah felt that the heels were perfect to complete her attire. Slipping on some dangling silver feather earrings, and a necklace to match, Hannah was ready.

Dinner was amazing. There were so many options and so many courses, Hannah thought she might need to take more walks around the ship. Thinking about walks around the ship made her smile in anticipation for the night. She couldn't help but look around the room to see if Chace was dining in the same lounge. All of her excitement made it hard to concentrate on eating.

"Hannah, what are you looking at?" asked Kaylee, trying to see what had caught her attention.

"Oh! Nothing. Sorry. Just staring at all the beautiful decorations," she fibbed blushing.

Hannah looked down at her unfinished Thai-style grilled chicken. She was way too full to eat another bite, but checking her phone she saw that it was only eight o'clock. She didn't want to show up too early and look desperate.

Hannah was so distracted that she barely noticed when Hunter leaned closer to her.

"You look really nice," he complimented, speaking soft enough that only she could hear. Kaylee and Aaron were on the opposite side of the table, and were chatting away about something they saw on deck four.

Hannah turned to say thank you and

almost knocked right into him. She didn't realize he had moved so close to her. His cologne smelled fresh and Hannah blushed.

"Thank you, Hunter," she responded, leaning back in her chair.

Hannah had to admit that he looked really good in his fitted gray blazer and silk tie. Normally, under any other circumstances, she would have loved all the attention he was suddenly giving her. Part of her did feel some flattery from it. But everything seemed more complicated now that Chace had entered the picture.

Hannah's attention was drawn back to the here and now when Kaylee and Aaron stood up from the table. Checking her phone for the fifth time, she now felt it was a good enough time to head to the promenade deck to meet up with Chace.

"Hannah, come over here for a minute?" asked Kaylee, gesturing for Hannah to follow her a few yards away from their table.

"I know that you're anxious to meet up with this Chace guy, but do me a favor, okay?" Kaylee asked. Hannah nodded.

"Please be careful," Kaylee pleaded with her eyes. Hannah hugged her sister and smiled.

"Thank you for caring. I promise nothing will happen that shouldn't happen," she replied, squeezing her sister's hand.

"And you better tell me *everything*!" Kaylee whispered. Hannah laughed and gave her a thumbs up before exiting the dining room in search of the elevator. Her heart was beating wildly as she got off on deck nine and went outside.

~~*~*~*

Chace made it to the stern around eight fifteen. He was leaning against the railing facing out to the dark sea. Talking to Hannah that morning had been amazing. He felt like he had known her much longer than a few hours. The fact that she had offered to meet up later made his day.

Behind him, Chace could hear the light clicking of heels coming toward him. Blowing out a breath of nervousness he turned around to see Hannah walking toward him. Her frame was silhouetted by a light shining from behind her.

As she got closer, Chace could make out her features more clearly. Her light blue dress blew softly in the chilled breeze in harmony with her stunning red hair. Her sweet smile made him feel like the luckiest man in the world.

"If I had known this was going to be a dress occasion, I would have put on something other than jeans and a hoodie," he teased, closing the gap between them. Hannah looked down at her dress and heels blushing.

"I guess I probably should have changed my shoes for the purpose of walking," she giggled.

"Well, if it's any consolation, you look very pretty," Chace complimented, raising his arm to rub the back of his neck.

"Thank you," she responded softly.

"So, I believe we were talking about where we grew up before you were summoned," he mentioned as they started walking. The light click-click of her heels kept the tempo of their walk.

"Yes, you had just told me that you lived in Nashville, Tennessee, but that you hadn't grown up there," recalled Hannah. Chace nodded.

"Right. So, I've lived in Nashville for about five years. I loved it at first, but then I found out last year that Madison, my younger sister, was having a baby and I started to get homesick. It would be my first time being an uncle. Her and her husband live in Raleigh, North Carolina where I grew up. I've been thinking about moving back," Chace explained, holding his hands behind his back.

"*Seriously?*" Hannah gasped, coming to a sudden halt. Chace turned to her confused, but nodding his head yes.

"That's crazy! I have lived my whole life in Charlotte!" exclaimed Hannah, her eyes wide.

Chace's jaw dropped.

"You're kidding me! That *is* crazy! My parents still live in Raleigh," Chace exclaimed, as they resumed their walk.

"My family used to go to Raleigh all the time when we were younger. We always went camping every summer at William B. Umstead State Park. It was beautiful. My parents had been camping there even before Kaylee and I were born," she said nostalgically.

"That's ironic. We use to go there, too. I loved the trails you could hike there. I'm surprised I never saw you," said Chace smiling. Hannah laughed.

"Well, you couldn't have missed me," she grinned, pointing to her hair.

"No, definitely couldn't miss you," said Chace softly.

He reached up and slipped a lock of her hair behind her ear. He felt her breathing speed up as her warm breath tickled his arm. It took all of his might not to touch her cheek. Chace decided that they should keep walking before he made a fool of himself.

Once back on track, the electricity from moments before had subsided. Being close to her was quickly becoming dangerous. He needed to be careful not to let his desires control his actions.

"Why did you move to Tennessee?" Hannah asked.

"There was a girl I had been dating around that time. She wanted to pursue a country music career. So, I followed my heart, at the time, and decided to make the move with her. At first it was okay, but we quickly grew apart and eventually ended up breaking it off. I stayed for four more years after the break up," he explained.

"What made you stay?" she asked. Chace could see he had her full attention.

"Well, I stayed because I wanted to see if I could try *my* luck in the music industry," he replied smiling. Hannah's eyebrows shot up in curiosity.

"Okay, my interests are really piqued now," she smiled, motioning him to continue the story. Chace chuckled. She looked cute when she was excited.

"Well, I like to think of myself as a singer-songwriter," he proclaimed.

"You sing?" Hannah asked, showing him her brightest smile. Chace's heart skipped a beat.

I'll juggle bowling pins with my eyes closed if it will keep her smiling at me like that, he thought.

"I've been known to dabble a bit with music. I learned how to play piano and guitar when I was young. When I moved to Tennessee, I started toying with the idea of making my own beats and writing my own songs. I discovered how to take popular songs and tweak the melody to make the song sound different but still recognizable," he explained.

"Is that easy to do?" Hannah inquired.

"It is complicated, but it's fun. And when you get it just right, it's one of the most satisfying feelings in the world," he declared.

"That's amazing that you know how to do that," she said astonished.

"I've recently started to upload some videos on the internet," he stated.

"Oh, how cool! Have you received a lot of feedback? Are you quickly making your way to stardom?" she asked jokingly.

"No, I don't see any red carpets for me in the near future. But you never know," he shrugged smiling.

"We've talked a lot about *me,* though. I feel like I'm hogging the limelight. I want to know more about Hannah Lane," said Chace, poking her in the arm playfully. She smiled timidly.

"What do you want to know?"

~~*~*~*

The conversation went on for almost two hours. Hannah told Chace about her childhood, her sister, her own love of music, and more. But she was starting to feel the ill effects of walking around the deck so long in heels. Her feet were becoming numb.

"I think I need to sit down for a moment," she announced, wobbling over to a nearby deck chair.

"Is everything okay?" asked Chace, taking a seat in the chair next to her. He turned his body so he was facing her.

"Yeah, I'm fine. I'm just being reminded of my decision to wear these tonight," Hannah replied, pointing to her heels.

"Ouch. You might want to take them off if it hurts to walk in them," he advised her. Slipping her shoes off, Hannah stretched out her pounding feet. The cool air blew across her toes and she sighed in relief.

"I want to see you again," voiced Chace, leaning his elbows on his knees. He moved closer to her. She looked into his eyes and momentarily forgot about her feet hurting. The pull of his stare drew her in like a moth to the flame.

"I'm sorry, what did you say?" she fumbled, trying to get control of her senses.

Chace chuckled. Reaching out, he gently took her hand in his, his thumb making circles on her skin. Sparks ignited underneath his touch.

"I said that I want to see you again," he repeated softly. Unable to find her voice, she looked up at him and smiled, nodding her head. He rewarded her with a dazzling smile.

If he keeps this up, I might die from heart failure, thought Hannah, breathing in slowly to compose herself.

"What do you have going on tomorrow?" asked Chace, releasing his grip on her hand. Her hand still tingled from his electrifying touch and she was saddened by the loss of their physical connection.

"The question is, what do you *want* to have going on tomorrow?" she inquired, dangling her heels in her hands by the deck floor.

"Well, I need to see you at least once during the day. And then I was hoping you would come with me to the Caliente Night Club," he offered, throwing out an idea.

Hannah bit her lip, looking down at the deck. She was not a dancer by any means and didn't want to embarrass herself, or Chace, by making a spectacle of herself. He seemed to read her hesitance and backtracked.

"But if you have other plans we can definitely work around your schedule," he commented quickly.

"No, that's not it. The thing is...I can't dance," she winced, looking up at him. She hoped that wouldn't put him off.

"You don't need to worry about that. You just move to the beat of the music. Nothing fancy. It'll be fun," he said smiling.

"Okay, I will give it a whirl," she sighed, standing up. She felt discomfort in the ball of her feet.

"From now on, when we do more walking, I won't wear heels," she cringed, bending down to rub one of her feet. Chace stood up next to her.

"You should probably be off your feet."

"Yeah, I think you're right," she agreed, walking inside. Each step felt like she was stepping on a jagged rock.

"Here, why don't you put your arm around my shoulders and let me support your weight," he instructed, taking her shoes from her injured hand. Hannah was going to protest, but taking another few steps proved to be almost unbearable.

"Okay, I'll take you up on your offer," she relented.

Chace came over to her side and she lifted her arm over his shoulders. She felt his strong arm slide around her waist to support her. The sparks she had felt when he touched her hand earlier were now magnified times one hundred. She felt her knees go weak.

"Easy there. I've got you," he encouraged, supporting her as her knees almost gave out. Hannah could feel her cheeks grow pink.

How embarrassing! How is he affecting me so much? she thought as they started walking.

His arm held her firmly as they rode in

silence down the elevator. Hannah looked up at him and saw that he was looking at her. Their eyes locked and all time stood still. If he didn't look away, she wouldn't be able to break their gaze. But the elevator dinged and broke the trance between them.

"Which way do we go?" he asked, looking left and right down the cabin hallway.

"Left," she pointed. Chace again supported her weight as they walked to her cabin.

"So did you want to do something tomorrow?" he asked as they neared her cabin.

"Yeah. Where do you want to meet up?" Hannah replied, trying to think of what there was that they could do on the ship.

"Why don't we meet in the atrium around noon?" Maybe we could do lunch?" he hinted.

"I would like that," she replied softly.
"Hannah, are you okay?" came a call from behind them. Hannah turned to see Kaylee, Aaron and Hunter approaching.

"Oh, yeah, I'm fine. Just sore feet," she answered. Kaylee looked from Hannah to Chace, a smile creeping onto her face.

"Kaylee, Aaron, this is Chace Devons. Hunter met him earlier today," said Hannah, glancing over at Hunter. His expression was sullen.

"It's nice to meet you, Chace. Beating up my little sister, are we?" joked Kaylee, reaching to take Hannah's shoes from his hand and shaking his hand in the process. Hannah's face flushed.

"No, she did this to herself. Two hours of walking in heels is apparently quite painful," he chuckled. Kaylee and Aaron laughed, but Hunter's eyes narrowed.

"Maybe you shouldn't have let her walk so much knowing that she had those heels on," he sneered, his steely gaze on Chace. Hannah's eyes widened at the accusation being hurled from Hunter.

"Oh, stop, Hunter. It's not his fault. Hannah's the goob who decided to do laps in these things," said Kaylee, presenting Hannah's heels.

"Okay, we can stop dogging on me now," said Hannah, shifting from one sore foot to the other. Kaylee giggled.

"Well, we are turning in for the night. See you for breakfast?" asked Kaylee, directing her attention to Hannah.

"Yes, I'll be there," she answered.

"It was nice to meet you. Thanks for helping my sister," said Kaylee to Chace, handing Hannah her heels.

"Not a problem," Chace smiled.

Kaylee and Aaron went to their cabin next to Hannah's. Hunter lingered in the hallway for a moment, looking between Hannah and Chace, before going into his cabin across the hall with a sigh.

"Well, that's the group," she said, taking out her cruise card to unlock her door.

"You and your sister look a lot alike," Chace pointed out.

"Yeah, it's really hard to miss a Lane," she giggled, shifting her weight to her other foot.

"Well, I want to hear more about the Lane's tomorrow. You, in particular," he winked.

Darn these feet! Hannah chided herself. If she hadn't been wearing those blasted shoes they may have had more of the night together.

"Tomorrow around noon?" he asked, leaning on her door frame. Hannah could only nod. Her thoughts were too jumbled to form a coherent response. Chace was so incredibly handsome.

"Well then, Miss Lane, I look forward to seeing you again," he smiled softly.

"As do I, Mr. Devons," Hannah smiled back.

Chace didn't move for a few moments. She thought he might kiss her. Her heart picked up speed as she thought of what his lips might feel like on hers.

"Good night, Hannah," he whispered, running the back of his finger down her cheek. Hannah felt a trail of fire left by his gentle touch.

"Good night," she said, biting her lip in a smile.

Slowly she closed the door until she heard it latch. She looked out the peep hole to see if Chace was still there. To her surprise, he was. He had a silly grin on his face. Hannah thought he looked so cute. She almost opened the door again, but knew that wouldn't be a good idea.

Just walk away, Hannah, she thought, coaxing herself away from the door. Curiosity got the best of her and she took one more look in the peep hole to see if he was still there. This time all she saw was an empty hallway.

About a half an hour later, Hannah had changed and washed up for bed. She felt anything but tired as she lay down on her bed and took out her journal. But before she could start her next entry, she heard a knock on her door.

Chace? she thought to herself. She got up and flew to the door. Opening it without looking, she saw her sister in the doorway. Hannah tried to keep the disappointment from showing on her face.

"Is this a bad time?" asked Kaylee. Hannah realized her attempt to fix her face had failed.

"No, silly. Come on in. Is everything okay?" she asked, moving aside to let Kaylee in.

"That's what *I* want to know about *you*. Give me the skinny on tonight!" Kaylee smiled brightly, propelling herself onto Hannah's bed. Hannah laughed and joined her sister in a less exuberant fashion. Her wrist was feeling better, but no need to press her luck.

Hannah recalled every moment of her time with Chace to her sister. By the time she finished, Kaylee was beaming from ear to ear.

"What are you smiling about? You have a crazy look on your face," laughed Hannah. Kaylee swatted her sister in the arm.

"He's it, Hannah," Kaylee proclaimed, losing none of her widespread smile.

"Um...you want to elaborate a little, sis?" asked Hannah, not understanding her sister's comment. Kaylee laughed lightly.

"You're going to marry him," she announced boldly.

Hannah could not believe what she was hearing. Marry him? She had not even known him for twenty-four hours.

"How many drinks did you have tonight, Kaylee?" she asked, looking at her sister like she had lost her marbles.

"Hannah, I'm serious! You should have seen the way he was looking at you when we showed up. That man loves you," stated Kaylee confidently. Hannah blushed at the thought of Chace liking her.

"And from your face I can tell that the feeling is mutual," Kaylee said winking. Hannah gawked at her sister.

"Kaylee, we've known each other less than a day. Are you some kind of fortune teller or something?" she questioned.

"You just watch. I was right about Hunter liking you, wasn't I?" she commented. That changed the topic.

"He looked mad when you guys came up to us," said Hannah, remembering the downward pull of his lips. Kaylee rolled her eyes.

"Hannah, don't worry about Hunter. I've known him as long as I've known Aaron. Hunter is someone who is used to getting what he wants. That was him pouting tonight. He's mad that Chace got to you first," she replied, waving off Hannah's concerns.

"You're crazy, you know that?" Hannah stated, getting up off the bed.

"Yes, I've been told that, but I know one

thing. Chace *will* ask you to marry him someday," she commented, waving her eyebrows up and down at Hannah as they walked to her door.

"Get out, you crazy loon," Hannah bantered, playfully shoving her sister out the door.

"You just wait and see," said Kaylee as she walked to her cabin. Hannah laughed, rolling her eyes.

"She is out of her mind," she laughed to herself as she went back to her bed. She was going to write in her journal, but it was getting late and Hannah was finally starting to feel sleepy. Plus, she needed to get to sleep soon if she didn't want to have bags under her eyes tomorrow.

Turning off the light, Hannah laid down and released a sigh. She fell asleep thinking about what the next day would bring.

~~*~*~*

Sleep evaded Hunter as his mind ran through the pictures of Hannah and Chace together earlier that night. When he, Kaylee and Aaron had gotten off the elevator, Hunter had seen someone down at their end of the hallway, but it was too far away to decipher who. But as they got closer he saw the light blue color of Hannah's dress. Her arm hung around Chace's shoulders and she was limping.

Hunter wanted to run up to her and push Chace aside, taking his place. Hannah was supposed to have her arm around *him*, not this newcomer.

He punched his pillow and turned over to his side. He wanted Hannah, and now that Chace was in the picture it was going to make things harder. But if he learned anything throughout life so far it was that determination payed off. He just had to be patient and wait for the right moment to intervene.

One thing he had to stop doing was acting like an idiot whenever he saw them together. He saw the way Hannah had reacted to him when he told Chace not to let her walk around in her heels. She looked shocked and a little miffed. That was not how he needed to handle those situations or she would grow to resent his presence.

You need to hold your tongue, he thought, scolding himself.

With his determination renewed, Hunter readjusted himself once more before eventually falling asleep.

December 23rd, 2018

The next morning at breakfast, Hannah was happy to see that Hunter didn't seem to be upset anymore. In fact, he was nicer than she had seen.

So what are your plans for the morning?" he asked her, taking a drink of his coffee. Hannah wiped her mouth and set her napkin down.

"Well, I planned on going to the internet lounge," she replied, leaving out the details as to why. Hunter looked at her strangely.

"We're on a cruise ship and you want to get on the internet?" he asked, almost laughing. Hannah smiled, shrugging her shoulders.

"She didn't say she was going to spend the day there," Kaylee smirked.

"Oh, ha ha," Hunter replied sarcastically. Kaylee stuck out her tongue. Hunter turned his attention back to Hannah.

"So I was wondering if you'd like to hang out sometime this morning?" he asked, looking at her with a hopeful expression.

Hannah felt trapped. She didn't know if she wanted to spend time with him alone. Briefly, she glanced at her sister with a pleading look. Thankfully, Kaylee took notice and spoke up.

"Why don't we all go up to the top deck and see what fun things there are to do up there?" she suggested, presenting a new idea. Hannah sighed inwardly for her sister's rescue. Hunter on the other hand didn't look too pleased. He looked like he wanted to object, but in the end he agreed to the idea.

Plans were made to meet at their usual spot around ten-thirty. When Hunter wasn't looking, Hannah mouthed the words "thank you" toward her sister. Kaylee winked and nodded her head.

Once the group dispersed, Hannah made her way to the internet lounge. Walking in, she noticed there was no one there. She knew there was some truth to what Hunter had said.

You wouldn't think of being on the computer when traveling on a luxury cruise, Hannah admitted to herself.

She found a computer facing away from the glass walls that made the room a fish bowl. Bringing up the search engine, Hannah typed two words into the search bar. Chace Devons. The internet loaded a moment before bringing her to a popular music website. There she saw his handsome face in a few different video options. It made her stomach do flip flops to think of knowing someone that other people had watched on the internet.

After plugging in her headphones, she clicked on the first video that came up on the screen. She was familiar with the song, but this version was different.

Soft, eerie music flowed into her ear buds that gave her shivers. Hannah saw Chace's hands at a keyboard. His face entered the screen and her heart skipped a beat. He was wearing black studio headphones and a round microphone stood in front of him.

And then the most magical thing happened that Hannah's ears had ever heard. Chace started to sing. Her eyes grew wide as she listened to him sing his version of the famous song. His expressions were so passionate, like every word had a deep meaning to it.

When he got to the chorus, his voice went into the most beautiful falsetto Hannah had ever heard. She sat there listening to his angelic voice with goosebumps on her arms. She couldn't believe the level of talent he had.

The second chorus started and gone was the soft falsetto. In its place was an edgy chest voice. Chace was a powerhouse and his notes were flawless. Hannah couldn't draw her eyes away from his face. Every word he sang was filled with so much zeal. He wore his heart on his sleeve when he sang, and she could feel his passion for music.

Hannah came to the last chorus of the song and couldn't remember how to breathe. His volume intensified with the song and an electric guitar had been added. With the amazing beat of the song, and the intensity of his voice, Hannah found herself without words. The end of the song made the hair on the back of her neck stand on end. Chace's vocal range was out of this world. His high notes in his chest voice were almost *too* perfect.

As the song came to an end, Hannah sat for a moment, staring blankly at the computer. She was about to unplug her headphones when she heard him start talking. Her eyes flashed back to the computer as he thanked everyone for listening and hoped that they liked his music.

Curious, Hannah scrolled down through the comments on the song. Many people, like her, were very impressed with the quality of his talent. People were asking for song requests for him to do. It made Hannah happy to know that people were appreciating his talent.

He'll get picked up real quick, she thought, continuing to scroll.

Some of the comments were from females fawning over how cute he was and how they loved him so much. She couldn't help but giggle at the comments that were over the top. But some of the girls that commented were very attractive and it kind of struck a cord with her.

Jealousy is a horrible feeling, she sighed, trying to shake off the unnecessary emotion. It's not like she had any rights to him. Yes, he seemed in to her, but who knew if that would go anywhere beyond a fling. That thought made her sad.

Shaking herself back to the present,

Hannah checked her phone for the time. It was ten twenty-five.

"Crap! I need to get down there," she panicked. Hannah unplugged her headphones and shut down the computer in a haste. She rushed down the hallway to the elevator. The last thing she needed was a lecture for being late again.

~~*~*~*

Hunter watched as Hannah got off the elevator and jogged toward them. She was smiling as she approached. He loved her smile. It made his insides melt.

"Hey, Hannah! You're on time," Kaylee jested. Hannah stuck her tongue out playfully at her sister.

"So, what are we doing?" asked Hannah.

"Well, we were thinking it might be fun to check out the mini golf course on the top deck," Kaylee suggested.

"That sounds fun. I haven't been to the top deck yet," voiced Hannah, nodding her head.

The top deck was breezy, but the weather was getting warmer the further south they went. They were around the west side of the Florida coast. Hunter followed the group as they retrieved their putters and golf balls. He couldn't remember the last time he had played a game of mini golf. To him it felt somewhat childish, but he would do it to be with Hannah.

He had been frustrated when Kaylee chimed in with a group activity after he asked Hannah if she wanted to hang out. What stung was that Hannah so readily agreed to what Kaylee offered instead of him.

Patience, he reminded himself.

The first few holes were fairly simple. Hunter and Aaron both made a hole in one on the second hole.

Hannah looked like she was having fun. It was a little challenging for her with her wrist not fulling functioning, but that didn't seem to bother her. Her hair blew softly in the wind. She looked so good in her snug jeans and dark blue t-shirt. Hunter couldn't help but take a few peaks at her backside when she would bend down to retrieve her ball.

By the end of the game, Kaylee ended up winning with the lowest score.

"That was fun!" Kaylee exclaimed, putting her putter back at the counter. Aaron laughed.

"Anything is fun when you win."

Hunter turned to see Hannah checking her phone for the fourth time. He was about to ask her if she wanted to grab a bite to eat with him, but she spoke before he had the chance.

"Well, I'm going to head off now. Kaylee, you're still going to do my hair later for the formal dinner, right?" she asked, looking at her sister.

"Yeah, I'll be at your room around five o'clock," stated Kaylee.

"Where are you off to, Hannah?" asked Aaron curiously. Hunter saw Hannah's cheeks grow pink, meaning only one thing. She was running off to see Chace again.

"Oh, Chace asked me to lunch," Hannah

answered, smiling sweetly. Hunter scowled inwardly. He was starting to hate Chace's name, especially coming from Hannah's lips. It was like a slap in the face.

"You sure have been spending a lot of time with him," said Aaron smiling. Hunter rolled his eyes.

"Yeah, he's really nice," she responded.

With that, Hannah headed down the stairs that led away from the top deck. Within moments, Hunter couldn't see her beautiful frame anymore.

"Want to talk?" asked Aaron from behind him. Hunter turned to see his best friend. He looked around and saw that Kaylee wasn't there.

"Kaylee went to use the restroom," said Aaron, answering Hunter's silent question. Hunter sighed, sitting down on a bench by the mini golf course. Aaron sat next to him with his head facing Hunter.

"I don't know, man," said Hunter, putting his face in his hands. Hunter had always felt so sure about everything. He never had trouble getting girls. He knew that Hannah had been into him at Aaron's wedding.

Probably might have been now had this Chace guy not ruined it, he thought bitterly.

"It's Hannah, isn't it," guessed Aaron.

"Okay, yes. I like her...a lot," he sighed, admitting the truth to his friend. It felt good to get it off his chest to someone.

"And I take it her new found interest in Chace doesn't sit well with you," Aaron guessed, cutting to the quick. Hunter looked at Aaron.

They had been best buds since elementary school.

"I don't know how to feel. I mean, I know I don't know much about Hannah, but I feel drawn to her. I've felt it since we met up at the airport. I get the feeling she *was* attracted to me, too, but then she met Chace and now she's almost awkward around me," said Hunter, looking down at the deck floor. He heard Aaron sigh.

"Listen, I love Hannah. She's like the baby sister I never had. You liking her is cool with me, but be careful. If she really is interested in Chace, you need to respect the decision she makes," Aaron cautioned.

Hunter knew his friend was right. He knew that he wasn't acting maturely about any of this. Something just came over him whenever he saw Hannah. He wanted her. Could he bury his brief feelings for her if she didn't choose him? That question left a sour taste in his mouth.

Kaylee returned and informed them that she was feeling a little nauseous and wanted to lay down. Aaron got up and accompanied his wife to their cabin. Hunter said he would meet up with Aaron later at his cabin in time for the formal dinner.

"I hope you feel better, Kaylee," Hunter called out. She turned around and smiled.

"Thanks, Hunter. I'm sure I'll be good. Just a little stomach ache," she smiled, holding her husband's hand.

Hunter sat on the bench for a few minutes more. He didn't want to go back to his cabin yet, but he wasn't sure what to do. Deciding he could use a walk in solitude, Hunter stood up and straightened out his pants. With no plan as to where he was going to walk, he set off, letting his feet take him where they may.

~~*~*~*

Hannah sat with Chace at the Lido Restaurant enjoying a pizza together. Being with him made her feel so good. They sat inside by a window looking out to sea.

"So tonight is the formal dinner. I take it you're going?" asked Chace, smiling at Hannah from across the small table. She bobbed her head up and down, finishing the bite of pizza in her mouth before answering.

"Yes, I'll be there. I did some serious shopping to find the formal dresses that I did," she declared, smiling before taking a drink of her water.

"Well, I'm anxious to see you in your dress. I'm sure you're going to catch the eye of every man in that room," he said, winking at her. Hannah flushed, biting her lip. He loved when she blushed. It made her face seem even more delicate than it was.

When he had touched her cheek the night before, he could feel her body's response. And he could feel the electricity created when his skin met hers. Chace had wanted to kiss her so badly, but shied away.

He wasn't one of those guys that dated a lot. Even in college there were only a few. The only serious relationship he ever had was with his ex, Lacy. He moved to Tennessee to be with her, and *that* was bold for him. But within a few months of him making such a huge commitment, that *she* had asked of him, he found Lacy in the arms of another man.

"Well, I don't know about *that*," said Hannah bashfully, bringing Chace out of his thoughts of the past. That was then and this was now, and the future looked a lot better with Hannah in his line of vision.

"Kaylee's going to do my hair in this really pretty braid that she learned from our mom," she mentioned excitedly, twirling a strand of her hair.

"So, not to bring the mood down, but I've noticed you mention your mom in past tense," said Chace. Hannah looked out the window for a minute and he immediately regretted bringing up such a personal topic. But she turned back toward him and offered a half smile.

"My mother passed away when I was thirteen. She was in a really bad car accident. They had her stabilized briefly in the ambulance, but she didn't make it," she replied softly. Chace felt horrible for bringing it up.

"Hannah, I'm sorry. I shouldn't have said anything," said he, trying to pull his foot out of his mouth. But she shook her head no.

"Honestly, it's okay. Toward the beginning of it all I couldn't talk to anyone about it. Not even Kaylee. Time heals most wounds. It doesn't hurt anymore, but the scar will always be there. I don't mind talking about it," she replied.

Chace threw their trash away led

Hannah out to the deck. The breeze was warm and it felt nice being outside.

"I thought the phrase was time heals *all* wounds," he said, looking down at Hannah.

"Yes, that is the popular saying. My dad would beg to differ, though," she said, the edges of her lips pulling downward.

Good going, Chace. Just keep twisting that knife, he thought, mentally slapping himself.

"We don't have to talk about it, Hannah," he stated, trying to rewind. Hannah turned toward the railing of the ship. She leaned her arms on the railing and looked over to him. Her eyes were open, honest and vulnerable. They spoke volumes about her integrity and sweet character.

"I can tell you. I have no secrets," she said, placing her hand on top of his. The sensation her touch gave him was palpable. He moved his thumb up to touch her finger, encouraging her to keep going.

~~*~*~*

Hannah hadn't talked about her parents to anyone, besides her sister, for a long time. The thought of her parents used to make her cry on the spot, but as she got older, she was able to live with the loss and eventually move on. She felt comfortable telling Chace about this part of her past.

"When my mom died, I think my dad died, too," she began.

"My father lived for my mother. She was

his whole world. They had both moved from Ireland when they were teens. They ran away from their family and eloped, sailing to the states to start a new life out of their families shadows.

"My mother was seventeen and my father was nineteen. Eventually they became citizens, but life for them was tough. Neither had any college experience and after only a year of being married, Mom became pregnant with Kaylee.

"My father look a job in construction. He wanted to make sure my mother never had to worry about what they would eat the next day.

"Four and a half years later they had me. By then, my parents were well established in Charlotte. My mother would make jewelry and sell them at local shops. She didn't do it for money. She did it because it was fun for her.

"Fast forward thirteen years, I was in junior high and Kaylee was a junior in high school about to graduate a year early. By then she was dating Aaron. That's when the accident happened.

"After the accident, my father was never the same. Over time he began missing work and eventually losing his job altogether. Bills weren't getting paid and we were barely making it by. One day, about six months after my mother passed, I came home from school and found Kaylee crying in the living room. She was holding a piece of paper stating that our house was in foreclosure. Being fourteen I didn't know what that meant.

"She told me to pack up what I could and

that we were going to stay with Aaron for the time being. Kaylee was eighteen by then and legally able to take care of me. But that didn't come without a burden. Kaylee was going to college and Aaron was in his last year of business school. Kaylee had to be the one to help me with homework, take me to volleyball practices, and console me when I got my heart broken," Hannah laughed at the part.

"Why did she have to do all that? Wasn't your dad there?" asked Chace confused. Hannah pursed her lips in frustration, looking out at the ocean.

"No. No, he wasn't there. Also in the letter about the foreclosure was a note from our father stating that he couldn't handle being around us anymore. Not that he didn't love us, but that we looked too much like Mom and that it killed him to see her every day in us.

"He ended up moving back to Ireland and we haven't heard from him since. He didn't get to see me graduate. Kaylee didn't have him to walk her down the aisle at her wedding...He missed everything," she answered bitterly.

A few moments of silence passed. Hannah assumed Chace was taking it all in. She didn't want him to feel sorry for her, because she was okay.

"You know, Kaylee isn't the only one who had to grow up fast," said Chace, looking down at her.

"What do you mean," she asked, confused.

"You did, too. Even though you had Kaylee to take care of you, I'm sure you gained a lot more independence than a girl at that age had to experience," he stated, rubbing her hand with his finger. Hannah had been so absorbed in telling him about her parents that she forgot her hand was on top of his. The movement of his thumb was both soothing and shocking.

"Maybe, but Kaylee and I have a really tight bond because of what we went through. We were close before all that happened, but it grew stronger after my mother died. I grew really close to Aaron, too. He became the big brother and helped Kaylee and I with everything. They were my rock," said Hannah, her voice quivering on the last word.

Don't cry, Hannah! You just got done telling him you were okay with everything, she scolded herself.

Suddenly, Chace pulled her close. Her face met with his shirt as he wrapped his arms around her.

"I'm sorry, Hannah," he whispered, his breath on her neck. Hannah sucked in a breath as her skin tingled. Being that close to him was ridiculously satisfying. Reluctantly, she slowly pulled back from the embrace. Chace's hand slid down her arm and softly gripped her hand.

"Thanks for listening," she commented, smiling as she wiped away her tear with the palm of her free hand.

"Thank *you* for sharing something so personal. I feel honored to know such a woman," he complimented, pulling her back toward the deck to walk. Hannah laughed lightly. She couldn't help the smile creeping onto her face. Chace hadn't let go of her hand.

After an amazing afternoon with Chace, Hannah walked back to her cabin. It was getting close to dinner and she needed to see Kaylee. Hannah knocked on their cabin door and Aaron opened it.

"Hey, Hannah. Kaylee's doing her hair. Do you want to come in?" he asked, opening the door wider. Hannah nodded and proceeded into the room. It smelled like Kaylee's favorite hairspray.

"I'm in here," Kaylee called from the bathroom. Hannah wandered in. Kaylee had French braided her hair and wrapped it in a twist at the nape of her neck.

"Wow! You look great! I'll never understand how you can French braid your own hair. I fail miserably every time I try," Hannah admitted, toying with one of the bobby pins on the bathroom counter.

"Some things you get, some things you don't," Kaylee jested.

"Did you want to do my hair here, or in my cabin?" she asked, looking at the clock on the wall. It was almost five o'clock. Kaylee shoved one more bobby pin in her hair and looked at her work. Satisfied, she turned to Hannah and smiled.

"Let's go to your cabin. I think Hunter is coming over here," Kaylee replied, gathering up her hair products. Hannah took some items Kaylee dumped in her arms. With all the products she was bringing, Hannah felt like she was getting ready to meet the Queen.

As they opened the door, Hunter was standing out in the hall about to knock.

"Hey, Hunter," greeted Kaylee cheerfully.

"Hey. Are you feeling better?" he asked. Hannah looked at her sister perplexed.

"I'm fine," assured Kaylee, looking at Hannah and then nodding her head to Hunter. He smiled to Kaylee and looked over to Hannah.

A range of different emotions played across his face before he settled with a smile. Not quite the same as the one he presented to Kaylee. Nevertheless, Hannah smiled and waved as she walked by him into the hallway. Kaylee followed behind her as Hannah opened her door.

"Catch you guys later," said Kaylee to Aaron and Hunter.

Walking to Hannah's bathroom, they both unloaded all of Kaylee's hair products onto the counter.

"Am I really going to need all of this stuff?" she inquired, picking up a jar of cream that smelled strange.

"Nah, but I took everything so if I needed something I wouldn't have to go back and forth to get it," Kaylee answered, motioning for her to sit.

For the next forty minutes Hannah's hair was subjected to many different sprays. She sat perfectly still with a face mask on that Kaylee had recommended she try. She felt like a life sized Barbie at the hands of a curious child. But she knew Kaylee was a professional.

"Alright! I think we're done," she announced, spraying Hannah's hair once more. Hannah coughed.

"If you spray any more of that stuff in my

hair, it'll never move again," she commented, waving her hand in front of her face.

"Oh, stop! It wasn't *that* much!" Kaylee countered.

She had Hannah facing away from the mirror for the last twenty minutes of her styling. Kaylee slowly peeled the mask off of Hannah's face and applied a thin layer of face cream.

"You're going to let me do my makeup, right?" asked Hannah grimacing.

"Yes, that's all you. I need to get back to my room so I can get my dress on. See you in a few," said Kaylee, heading to the door.

"I'll pick up my stuff later," she called as she closed the door. Hannah turned around to look at her bathroom counter. It was covered with hair and facial products.

She'd better come back later, she thought sighing. Hannah looked up at her reflection and felt her mouth pop open. Her hair was beautiful! It looked like something out of a magazine. Strands of her hair dangled down her neck, and her face had a soft glow from the mask and cream Kaylee had applied.

You outdid yourself this time, Kaylee, she thought, looking at her hair from different angles.

Remembering she only had a little bit of time left, Hannah scurried to her closet. There were two formal dinner nights on the cruise, so she had packed two evening dresses. One was an emerald green backless halter top gown that fit snugly down the length of her body. It had a slit on the right side that went from her foot to her lower thigh.

The other dress was a black gown that went off the shoulders. The classy black dress hugged the curves of her body down to her knees. Tight long sleeves went from the middle of her upper arm down to her wrists. Hannah thought since it was getting close to Christmas that the green dress would be more appropriate.

After getting her dress on, Hannah picked some glossy heels that were the same color as her dress. She chose a pair of small ruby red earring studs encircled by tiny diamonds. The necklace that it came with had the same stones and was held by a delicate chain. The set had been a gift for Hannah to wear from Aaron for the wedding.

With the finishing touches of her makeup complete, Hannah stepped back from the mirror and gave herself a good look over. She smiled, feeling like a princess.

A knock came at her door.

"Coming," she called, closing up her makeup bag. Opening the door, she expected to see Kaylee. But to her surprise, she was face to face with Hunter.

~~*~*~*

Hunter was sure he was dreaming. Before him stood a goddess. Hannah's dark green dress was stunning. It hugged her curves perfectly. Her hair was braided and wrapped around her head like a crown while little wisps fell to her neck, gracing her delicate shoulders.

"Hannah, you look...Wow!" Hunter

stumbled over his words. Hannah blushed, looking down at her dress.

"Thanks, Hunter," she replied sweetly.

"Oh, Hannah! You look so beautiful!" Kaylee commented, coming out of her cabin.

"Thank you. And thank you so much for doing my hair. You did such a great job!" Hannah gushed.

"Hey, it's what I do for a living. You're lucky I don't charge you," Kaylee laughed.

"Well, come on, ladies. We need to get a move on if we're going to make it to dinner," stated Aaron, offering Kaylee his arm. She smiled lovingly up at him and put her hand through his arm.

Hunter looked down at Hannah and offered her his arm the same as Aaron had. Hannah hesitated a moment before slowly slipping her delicate hand through his arm. He tried to brush off her hesitation, but if he was honest with himself it stung.

"You look very nice tonight," Hannah complimented, looking up at him. Hunter looked down at her surprised.

"Oh, well, thank you. Gotta look good if I'm going to be standing next to an angel," he remarked, pulling her a little closer to him. Hannah blushed again. He was delighted to see that she didn't pull away from him. He felt a smile pull his lips upward. For the first time, Hunter felt like maybe he still had a chance with her.

Entering the dining room, Hunter could hear Hannah gasp. He looked down to see her staring at all the decorations and fancy tables in front of them. He liked that she was easily excited.

"Hey, guys, this is our table," Kaylee called behind her shoulder.

There was a large round table that could easily fit ten people. The red and green napkins were folded in a fancy style and there was an impressive Christmas centerpiece with a flickering candle. Aaron and Kaylee sat down first. Hannah sat next to Kaylee, leaving the seat to her left open for Hunter.

As dinner progressed, the conversation flowed smoothly between everyone at the table. After Hunter and his group had been seated, an older couple joined them followed by two talkative women, making their table full. Soft, jazzy Christmas music played as a low buzz of conversations emanated around the room.

Hunter turned to Hannah and tapped on her left hand. The loose hairs from her braid shifted gracefully as she turned to give him her attention. He was completely taken by her.

"What's up?" she asked, giving him a smile.

"I noticed you're not wearing your wristband tonight," he commented, running his pinky along her wrist.

"Oh yeah, I didn't think it would really go well with my dress so I thought I'd wing it tonight," she responded, pulling her hand away.

"Hannah, you need to try this fish! It's out of this world," Kaylee declared, taking Hannah's focus away from Hunter.

If I don't get her alone, I'll never have the chance to have her attention, Hunter silently complained. He took a bite of his lobster and started to think of ways he could steal a few moments alone with Hannah.

~~*~*~*

Chace sat at the formal dinner with the friends that he had come with on the cruise. He looked around the large room to see if he could spot Hannah. It took him a few moments before he finally found her. She sat a few tables away from him, her body partially facing in his direction. From his view, he could see she was wearing a dark green dress that appeared to be backless.

She is stunning! thought Chace, as he watched her talk animatedly with her sister. Hannah's smile lit up the room. It was like a ray from heaven shined down on her.

"What's got your attention over there, Chace?" asked his friend, Jake.

"Whatever, or *whoever*, it is must be pretty interesting," Lana, Jake's wife, smiled. Chace turned his attention back to his group and looked over to Jake.

"I'm sorry. What were you guys saying?" he asked apologetically. He knew he wasn't being the best of company right now as he ogled over at Hannah. Jake laughed.

"We were just wondering if you saw a tasty dish go by, or if a Siren had called to you," Jake observed, taking a drink of his wine. Chace smiled sheepishly at his friend.

"I think it's the latter of the two," mentioned the fourth participant of the group,

Dan, as he wiggled his bushy eyebrows up and down. Lana gasped, clasping her hands together in merriment.

"Who is she!?" she inquired, bouncing in her seat as she looked around the room.

"Is it this the girl that you've gone out of your way to see since the second day we set sail?" asked Jake.

"Yes, it's her," Chace admitted, his face getting warm.

"Where is she sitting?" asked Lana, looking around the room as though she was going to spontaneously combust.

"Honey, if you continue to shriek like that you're going to embarrass the poor guy," Jake commented, setting a hand on his wife's arm. Lana shooed him off and focused her attention back on Chace.

"Where is she sitting?" she asked again. Jake gave him an "I surrender" look, shrugging his shoulders. Taking a deep breath, Chace turned slightly and told Lana to look for a woman in a green dress with red hair. Lana looked a moment in the direction he was facing and he could tell when she spotted her.

"Chace, she's beautiful!" she declared happily. He smiled without turning his eyes from Hannah.

"And you've got it bad," Lana remarked. Chace couldn't disagree with her. Hannah was different then any woman he had ever met. She drew him in and he didn't know if he could get away. Not that he wanted to.

"So, are you going to go over there?" Dan asked, bringing Chace back to their conversation. Reluctantly, he took his eyes off of Hannah.

"And do what?" he asked sarcastically.

"I don't know. Say hi or something," Dan shrugged.

"No. See the guy she's sitting next to?" Chace asked, directing their attention back to Hannah's table.

"Yeah. Are they an item?" asked Dan.

"No, I don't think so, but I get the feeling that he doesn't like me hanging out with her," Chace observed.

When he looked back at Hannah, he saw that Hunter had asked her a question and was lightly running his finger across her wrist. Fire sparked in the pit of his stomach at Hunter's obvious attempt to flirt with her. He breathed a sigh of relief when Hannah moved her hand away from Hunter as she answered his unknown question.

"Well, if he doesn't have any claim on her then you don't have anything to worry about," answered Lana pointedly.

"Geez, Lana! What's gotten into you tonight? You're all fired up," Dan commented laughing.

Chace chuckled. He had known the threesome since he moved to Tennessee. They all worked at an accounting firm together. Chace knew a good part of the reason he felt he could stay in Tennessee after he broke it off with Lacy was because of them. Lana had even tried to hook him up with the receptionist at their work. Chace thought it was sweet, but the girl barely looked like she had graduated high school. What was he going to do, pass notes with her?

Then an idea struck him. He asked his friends if anyone had a pen and a piece of paper.

"I have some. Be thankful I brought my purse," she replied with a wry grin.

"Lana, you always have paper in your purse. Whenever you think of something you have to write it down then and there or you'll forget it," Jake joked.

Lana handed Chace the wallet sized notebook and a blue pen. He pursed his lips trying to think of something he could say to Hannah. With an idea forming, he began to write.

Chace reread what he wrote. He hoped it wasn't too cheesy. Folding it once, he looked around for a waiter. After a moment, he was able to flag one down. He gave the older gentlemen his note asking him to deliver it to Hannah, pointing out who she was. The waiter smiled and agreed, winking at Chace before he went on his way.

~~*~*~*

Hannah was in awe of the formal dinner. Everything was so beautiful and filled to the brim with holiday decor. The Christmas music playing in the background was so peaceful and relaxing that she often drifted from the conversations and just daydreamed. She thought of Chace and how she loved spending time with him. It frightened her a little at how quickly she was developing feelings for him.

I just have to keep myself in check, was what she told herself.

"Excuse me, Miss Hannah?" spoke a voice quietly behind her. She turned to see a waiter with lightly graying hair bending down toward her.

"Yes, that's me," she answered, turning toward him.

"I have been asked to deliver something to you," he stated, smiling at her.

Hannah looked at him befuddled. The waiter held out a small piece of paper that was folded in half. She took the paper from his hand and thanked him. He winked at her as if he was keeping a secret and walked away.

Hannah unfolded the paper in her lap curiously.

'Come what sorrow can,
It cannot countervail the exchange of joy,
That one short minute gives me in her sight'

Look back to your right

Hannah did as the note instructed and looked behind her. She didn't know who, or what, she was looking for. Sweeping her eyes around the room, she found who she believed had sent the sweet poem. There in her line of vision was Chace. He was a few tables back from her.

She caught his eye and her heart raced as he gave her a heart-stopping smile. Hannah returned the smile and held up her finger to tell him to hold on. Chace nodded his head and turned back to the group at his table.

Hannah turned her attention to Kaylee.

"Kaylee, do you have a pen by any chance?"

Kaylee looked over at her with an apologetic look on her face.

"No, I'm sorry, Hannah. Why do you need one?" she asked. Hannah smiled and showed her the note Chace had had delivered to her. Kaylee's eyes grew wide as she looked behind her.

"Kaylee, don't look!" Hannah whispered embarrassed. She looked back and was thankful that Chace wasn't looking in their direction.

"Chace sent you this?" she asked excitedly. Hannah bobbed her head up and down, making Kaylee laugh.

"Let me ask Aaron if he has a pen," she stated, turning to her husband. When he shook his head no, Hannah was getting a little down.

How and I supposed to write him back if I can't find a pen? she thought frantically.

"I'm sorry to have been eavesdropping, but did you say you needed a pen?" asked a woman across the table. Hannah looked up at her and nodded hopefully.

"Here, you can have this one," offered the woman kindly. Hannah thanked her and looked down at the paper Chace had sent her.

What should I write? she thought, tapping her cheek with the pen.

"What are you going to say back?" asked Kaylee, echoing Hannah's thoughts.

"What, besides the word *blush*?" laughed Hannah. Kaylee smiled and rolled her eyes.

"Honestly, Hannah! Didn't you ever study Shakespeare?" she scolded.

"Well, yes, but I don't know a poetic response to something like *this*!" she responded, pointing to the note.

"I can't help you there," said Kaylee, turning back to her food, leaving Hannah to her thoughts.

Just write what comes to your mind, she told herself. Making some space below his words, Hannah started to write.

Had I known dinner was going to involve Shakespeare, I would have studied. Very smooth, Rico Suave.

Hannah smiled, satisfied with her note, and folded the piece of paper back along the same crease. Now it was Hannah's turn to look for a waiter to pass the note back to Chace. A waitress came to the opposite side of her table.

"Excuse me, can I ask you a question, please?" she asked to the young Hispanic waitress. She smiled and came over to Hannah's side of the table.

"I help you, miss?" she asked in broken English.

"Yes, can you please give this to a man named Chace? He is at that table over their, sitting closest to us. See, he just took a drink," Hannah pointed. The waitress smiled.

"I take to him," she agreed, taking the note.

Hannah watched as the waitress made her way to Chace's table. She breathed a sigh of relief when the girl handed the note to him. She saw him smile and peek back. He winked at her before turning back around to read her missive. Hannah giggled, feeling like she was in junior high writing a note to her crush.

Within moments she looked up to see a different waitress coming to her side and giving her the same piece of folded paper. Hannah thanked her and quickly opened the note below the table.

'Though this be madness, yet there is method in 't'

Meet me outside the dining room entrance

Hannah's heart skipped a beat. She looked behind her to see if Chace was looking at her, but instead found he wasn't at the table anymore. At his table, she saw a woman with jet black hair pulled up in a bun looking at her with a smile. The woman pointed toward the entrance of the dining hall exactly where Chace had said to meet him. Hannah flushed. The woman must have been part of Chace's party, and was clearly in on it.

"Where did he go?" asked Kaylee, interrupting her thoughts. Hannah showed her the response from Chace and smiled widely.

"What are you waiting for? Go, silly!" Kaylee responded, playfully shoving Hannah's arm.

"You're leaving?" asked Hunter. Hannah looked over at him and nodded.

"Would you like me to take you back to

your cabin?" Hunter asked, moving his chair back to stand. Hannah grabbed his arm and pulled him back down to sit.

"No, Hunter, you don't need to do that. But thank you for the offer," she responded, letting go of his arm. The note in her hand slipped out and floated to the table. Hunter glanced down at it. She snatched the note quickly, hoping he hadn't seen any of it.

"See you guys later," Hannah announced quietly to her group as she stood up from her table. Hunter rose up with her. He looked like he was going to follow her, but as she walked away he just watched. Hannah turned her attention back to the dining room entrance. Her heart picked up speed as she neared the double doors.

~~*~*~*

Chace stood a few feet away from the doors. He looked around as people meandered through the hallway. He heard the quiet click of a door from behind him and turned to see the woman who had starred in his dreams the previous night. Hannah smiled at him radiantly.

"I'm glad you came," he stated, reveling in her vast beauty. He still couldn't believe she was real. But there she was standing in front of him, smiling at *him*.

"Well, with Shakespearian lines like that, what girl wouldn't come to meet you?" Hannah joked, holding up the note they had passed to each other.

"How did you pull those quotes out so

quickly?" she asked in amazement.

"My parents are huge Shakespeare fans. I grew up hearing all the plays, memorizing some of the acts for prizes, all that stuff. I guess all that hard work stuck with me," he answered, shrugging his shoulders.

"Very impressive. Question though," Hannah started.

"Shoot," he replied, giving her the go.

"Who is the lady at your table with black hair?" Hannah inquired. Chace grinned, shaking his head.

"I'm fairly sure you're referring to my friend's wife, Lana. Why? What did she do?" he asked, grimacing at what face she may have given to Hannah, or if she had spoken to her.

"I looked over at your table after you sent your last note. I was going to nod my head yes to you, but you had already slipped out. So instead of seeing you, I caught her eye. She smiled at me and pointed to the exit you had just told me to go to," Hannah explained.

Chace smirked and rolled his eyes.

"Lana is a great person. She has always wanted to see me happy with someone, especially after what my ex had done," he said, starting to walk. He reached out behind him and offered Hannah his hand. She took it willingly with no hesitation, making his heart swell.

He led Hannah to a small seating area a few yards away from the dining room. There were couches and soft plushy chairs for people to put their feet up and relax. The room was open to the hallway, but it was private enough to have a conversation.

Chace motioned for Hannah to take a seat on one of the couches. She chose a couch toward the window. Even though it was dark, there were lights that could be seen from outside on the deck.

"I'm glad I could steal you away for a moment," said Chace, sitting down next to her. He turned his body toward her so he could see her better. Hannah did the same, pulling her slim legs up and tucking them under her silky green evening dress. He longed to reach out and touch her.

"You know, honestly, I'm glad you did. If I were to eat one more bite I would have probably needed to put on my fat pants," she joked, putting her hand up to her flat stomach.

"*You* have fat pants?" he laughed, raising his eyebrows.

"Well, they're not actually fat pants. Kaylee and I joke about having to wear fat pants when we've eaten too much. Really they are just like sweat pants. Something to give us some extra comfort room," she explained.

"I was going to say, there is no way *you* could ever need anything with the title of *fat* in it," Chace smiled, sweeping his hand in the air around her body. Hannah laughed and tucked a piece of her loose hair behind her ears.

"I definitely got my mother's genes," she stated.

"Well, your mother must have been a beautiful woman," he complimented, earning a glowing blush from Hannah.

"Thank you. And she was. I'll have to

show you a picture of her sometime. I have one on my phone, but it's not with me," she said, holding her hands in the air.

"And neither is your wrist bandage. I'm glad to see that it's healing," said Chace, lightly pulling her left hand toward him. He ran his fingers along her small wrist softly. Goosebumps raised along her arm and he smiled, looking up at her. Hannah laughed, pursing her lips.

Chace and Hannah talked for a while before they started seeing people in evening attire trickle out of the dining room. One of the people he recognized was Hunter. Chace had seen Kaylee and Aaron walk ahead of him, but they were in deep discussion over something and didn't notice them. Hunter, however, did notice.

The look on Hunter's face was irrefutable. Fire burned in his eyes as he looked at Chace and noticed his hand holding Hannah's. There wasn't a doubt in his mind that Hunter had feelings for her.

Hannah's position froze when she caught a glimpse of Hunter. Chace looked over to her and saw trepidation in her eyes. He looked back to Hunter and squeezed her hand lightly for assurance. He didn't know what for, but somehow he felt that she needed it.

Hunter looked down at the floor and then back up at them one last time before walking away.

"Hannah?" said Chace, pulling lightly on her hand. Shaking her head, she turned toward him. The look in her eyes read uncertainty.

Is there something going on between

Hannah and Hunter? There couldn't be. She's sitting here with me holding my hand, he thought, trying to ease himself.

"Is everything okay?" he asked. Hannah blew out a breath, closing her eyes.

"Yeah, everything is alright," she smiled, opening her eyes to him.

Chace narrowed his eyes slightly. He wasn't fully buying it. Hannah bit her lip, looking down at her dress. He moved closer to her on the couch to where their knees were touching and her attention was brought back to him.

"Hannah, has Hunter hurt you?" he asked, praying that wasn't the case. Hannah's eyes grew wide.

"No, of course not. He's just makes me feel uncomfortable sometimes," she admitted.

Chase exhaled slowly. He was never much of a fighter and wasn't one to believe that solved anything. But he would if it meant he was standing up for Hannah.

"Do you mind if I ask what makes you uncomfortable?" he asked.

"Kaylee said that Hunter is someone used to getting what he wants. She says he likes me. I don't know how much I believe that, but he has been acting strange around me and asking if I'd hang out with him. Thankfully, whenever he's asked, Kaylee has been there and has bailed me out. He's a good guy, I just don't like him like that," Hannah explained, fiddling with her dress.

"No offense, but it is very obvious that Hunter is into you. But if he's bothering you, then you might want to tell your sister or brother-in-law," Chace advised.

"Well, so far it hasn't been anything I can't handle. I just don't feel like I want to be alone with him," she stated.

"I don't want you to be alone with him either," he winked, lightening the mood. Hannah giggled shoving him in the arm. Chace caught her as she was retreating and pulled her up playfully. He held her arm as she steadied herself.

"Sorry. I forgot you were in heels," he said sheepishly.

"No sweat. I kind of forgot, too," she admitted.

Chace took a moment to study Hannah as she stood in front of him. He loved that shade of green on her. It made her eyes pop. The delicate jewelry she wore made her seem even more exquisite. He stepped closer to her until they were only a foot apart.

"Hannah, you are the most beautiful woman I have ever seen," he spoke softly. He brushed the back of his hand against the peddle soft skin of her cheek. Hannah breathed in heavily as her eyes drifted closed. Her head leaned into his hand.

Kiss her! his mind screamed. Chace's brain whirled. Oh, how he wanted to kiss this red headed beauty, but as usual when getting to this stage with a girl he liked, he froze.

Hannah opened her eyes and looked at him sweetly. A pinch of pink graced her cheeks as she smiled up at him.

"Thank you, Chace Devons," she

whispered. Her eyes smiled up at him as if they were dancing.

"Any time, Hannah Lane," he replied, stepping back a bit.

"So are you still wanting to go dancing tonight?" she asked, grimacing playfully.

"Don't think you're getting out of it that easily," he commented, wagging his finger at her. Hannah giggled and sighed.

"Your funeral," she said, shrugging her shoulders as she headed for the hall. Chace laughed, catching up to her as she went to the elevator. He slowed just a little to take in the view of her backless dress. Her creamy skin looked flawless sprinkled with a smattering of small freckles.

Hannah and Chace got on the elevator together and discussed where they were meeting up and when. The doors opened to his floor first. He took her hand and brought it to his lips, kissing her skin softly.

"See you soon," he whispered.

~~*~*~*

Hannah dressed in a daze. Slipping into a pair of jean shorts and a white T-shirt, she felt much more comfortable. She loved wearing her evening dress, but was happy to be in flexible clothing. Even though she was nervous about going to the Caliente Dance Club tonight, almost all thoughts of that were washed away when she thought of Chace being there.

Her hand still burned from where he had kissed it. His lips were so smooth on her skin, she had almost fainted at the tenderness.

Heading out her door, Hannah went to Kaylee's room and knocked on the door. Kaylee opened the door, her hair a messy wreck. Her face was pale and her forehead had a light sheen of sweat.

"Kaylee! What happened?" Hannah asked, inviting herself in. Kaylee closed the door and sat down on her bed wearily.

"I'm fine, Hannah. Just a little sea sick, I guess," she smiled faintly. Hannah thought that was strange. She hadn't felt the ship moving much at all.

"Where's Aaron?" she asked.

"He went to get me some Sprite," Kaylee replied.

"Do you want me to stay with you until he gets back?" Hannah wanted to know. Kaylee waved her hand shooing her away.

"If I am sick, I don't want you anywhere near me. Aaron can take care of me. I'm sure it's something I ate that doesn't agree with me," Kaylee reassured. Hannah didn't want to leave her sister alone. She checked the time on her phone and knew she needed to meet Chace at the dance club soon.

"Meeting up with Chace?" Kaylee asked smiling.

"Yeah, he wants me to go to the Caliente Dance Club with him," Hannah said sourly. Kaylee laughed, holding her stomach carefully.

"Boy is he in for it," she commented. Hannah smirked.

"Okay, I'm not *that* bad," she remarked, putting her hands on her hips.

Before Kaylee could reply, Aaron came through the door, holding a Sprite and a bag of crackers.

"Hey, Hannah. Did Kaylee come get you?" he asked, looking worriedly at his wife. Hannah shook her head.

"No, I was just coming over to tell her where I would be tonight in case you guys needed to find me," she informed him.

"Hannah, please don't worry about me. I'm fine. I've been sick before and I'll be sick again. Just go have fun and don't step on his feet," Kaylee joked. Aaron looked at Kaylee curiously.

"Thanks, Kaylee. See you later," Hannah waved as she made her exit.

The Caliente Dance Club was easy to find. Hannah could hear the music coming from behind the door and she stopped for a moment. Did she really want to do this? Doubt clouded her thinking as she bit nervously on her bottom lip.

"Hopefully you're not thinking of ditching me in that pretty little head," stated a voice behind her. Hannah smiled and turned to see Chace. He had changed into jeans and a red and white stripped shirt.

"Not ditching *you*. Just the club," she answered, jutting her thumb toward the doors. Chace shook his head.

"No, you don't. Trust me, it's not as hard as you're making it out to be," he said, taking her hand and leading her in.

The music was deafeningly loud compared to the quietness of the hallway. Blue and red lights flashed around to the beat of the music. She could feel the beat thumping in her chest. Everywhere arms were swinging in the air and body's swayed every which way. Hannah thought it was a little out of Chace's character to be into stuff like this.

He led her to the bar and told her he would be back in a moment. Hannah watched curiously as he faded into the crowd. She took a seat at one of the barstools and continued to watch the crowd of dancers.

"Hannah?" shouted a voice to her right. Looking over she saw Hunter a few seats down with a beer in his hand. He made his way over to her, smiling and stumbling a little on his way.

"What are you doing here?" he asked loudly over the music.

"I'm here with Chace," she stated. Hunter's face turned sour, but Hannah could also see a hint of sadness in his eyes.

"Well, I don't see him. Want to dance with me?" he asked, taking a rather large gulp of his beer.

"Um, thanks, but I don't really like to dance," Hannah answered lamely. Hunter looked at her with his eyebrow raised and then pointed to the dancing mob of people. She knew what he was referring to.

"Come on, Hannah! Come dance with me," he shouted a little too loudly, emptying his drink in one mouthful. A few people at the bar turned their attention to them. She began to protest, but Hunter grabbed her wrist and started to pull her toward the dance floor.

"Hunter, no, really. I don't want to. Ouch!

You're hurting my wrist!" she shouted, trying to free herself. Hunter stopped at the fringe of the dance floor and turned toward her.

"Why not, Hannah? I thought you liked me," accused Hunter. He was still grasping her wrist. Hannah looked around to see if anyone was witnessing their conversation.

"Hunter, this really isn't the place to talk about this. Please, let me go," she pleaded. Hunter looked at her with consternation etched in his eyes.

"Okay, Hannah. But I want to have a chance to talk to you sometime," he relented, still holding on. Suddenly, Hannah saw someone's hand grab Hunter's wrist forcefully.

"Let go of her now!" Chace demanded in a dark tone. Hannah eyes went wide in surprise at the fierceness of Chace's voice, his hard like flint. Hunter glared at him with fire in his eyes, but slowly released Hannah's wrist. He looked once more at Hannah and his face softened momentarily before he turned and disappeared into the crowd.

"Hannah, is everything okay?" asked Chace firmly.

Hannah nodded and walked back over to the bar with Chace. Once again she sat down on one of the barstools. She held her wrist tenderly. It hurt from Hunter's force. Chace came up in front of her. She knew he was looking at her wrist being coddled by her other hand. His eyebrows pulled downward as he gently took her wrist into his hand.

"What happened?" he asked, his tone edgy.

"He spotted me sitting at the bar and came over to ask me to dance. I told him no. He looked like he had been drinking. Anyway, he tugged me out toward the dance floor. He grabbed my injured wrist," she explained as Chace lightly rubbed her wrist.

"Are you okay?" he asked, looking her straight in the eyes. Hannah nodded and could see him visibly relax.

"Okay, everyone, as many of you may know tonight at Caliente we are going to do something a little different," the DJ announced over a loud speaker. Everyone in the crowd looked to one another. Some seemed to know what was going on. Others, like Hannah, looked around confused.

"Well, for those of you joining tonight on a whim, you're in for a treat. Tonight is our Karaoke night. Along with our upbeat dance music we are going to intermix special requests from the crowd. So could everyone give it up for our first singer, Chace Devons!" called the DJ as the crowd clapped.

Hannah whirled around to Chace. He was looking at her beaming from ear to ear. She hadn't noticed when he showed up before that he had a microphone in his hand. Hannah's eyes grew large as he squeezed her hand before weaving her through the mass of people to the stage. He let her go before he hopped up onto the platform and took a seat on the stool center stage.

"Hey, everyone. This song is a little different then your typical Karaoke song. You'll probably know it, but it's a slightly different version from the original. Hope you guys enjoy it," he spoke confidently into the mic.

Hannah could hear people around her murmuring and whispering about what it could be. Chace turned to the DJ and nodded for him to start the song.

Only a beat into the song Chace began to sing. The lyrics of the song sounded familiar, but the arrangement that he sang kept the song a mystery. Hannah didn't care. Her eyes were glued to Chace. His gaze was fixed solely on her, his eyes closing momentarily, accentuating his passion.

Hannah could hear harmonies of himself in the song as she had when she listened to his song earlier that day on the internet. Chace had made this song, and more importantly, he had brought it with him tonight with the intention of singing it to her. Her heart felt like it was going to explode.

Into the chorus, Hannah started to recognize what the song was. It was 'Kiss The Girl' from the Disney movie, The Little Mermaid. That had been one of her favorite Disney movies growing up. She always pretended she was Ariel because she had red hair like the Disney princess.

The melody of the song was mysterious and dark. It gave it a completely different sound. This version made it sound more mature. And watching Chace sing it made it a whole different world of its own. Everyone in the room swayed back and forth as he continued.

"I think he's looking at her," spoke a girl to her left. Hannah didn't look, but she knew the *her* they were referring to. She kept her focus on Chace as the song came to an end. Cheers erupted throughout the club as he set the microphone on the stool and nodded to the crowd with a smile. The DJ came around to pat him on the back and handed him his thumb drive back.

Chace turned toward the crowd and spotted Hannah. He smiled and jumped off the stage heading toward her. Stopping in front of her, he held out his hand for her to take. Blushing, she took it as he pulled her closer.

"Kiss her! Kiss her!" chanted the audience loudly. Hannah bit her lip as Chace looked down at her. Was he going to kiss her? He leaned closer to her and she could hear her blood pumping in her ears. The crowd continued to get louder as Chace's face got closer to hers. But he veered to the right of her face and closed in on her ear. His breath tickled her ear as he spoke softly to her.

"Come with me."

Instantly, he ran through the mob with Hannah trying to keep up with him. She would have lost him had she not been attached to his hand. All the girls in the room called out "Aww!" and "That's so cute!" as Chace and Hannah ran past them.

Finally making it out the door and around the corner from the dance club, Chace stopped, causing Hannah to almost collide with him.

"What are we..." she started before he put his finger up to her lip.

"Just follow me," he answered, walking

quickly toward the elevator. They stood in silence as the elevator took them up to the top deck.

After reaching their designated floor, Chace continued to lead her to the deck outside. The air was warm and smelled of sea salt. It blew through Hannah's wavy hair that she had taken down from the formal dinner.

Chace took her up a few stairs and stopped at a mid deck lounge area. He smiled down at her and walked her to a secluded section of the deck with an inviting, over-sized, plush turquoise lounge chair. Tiki torches were lit on either side and a wood slatted wall separated them from the rest of the deck.

Hannah took a seat and moved herself to the back of the chair. There was still plenty of room for Chace and probably more. He moved close to her. The dim light from the tiki torches touched his face and Hannah could see he was looking at her.

"Chace, that song you sang...your voice...it was so..." she stumbled over her words. She couldn't get the right words out to express how heartfelt that song was. Chace chuckled, running his fingers through his hair.

"So you liked it?" he asked, situating himself to face her.

"Liked it? That was amazing! You have so much talent, Chace!" she proclaimed exuberantly.

This time it was Chace's turn to blush. He looked down at her hands in her lap and took one. She moved a little closer to him so her arm didn't have to stretch uncomfortably.

"The lyrics of that song are very applicable to me," he stated, drawing figure eights on Hannah's hand.

He looked up at her and this time Hannah saw a different look in his eyes. She saw longing and desire. Her breath caught in her throat at what he was hinting toward. He leaned forward slowly, closing the gap between them. When his face was inches from hers, he started to sing softly to her the words he had sung in the club, his lips almost making contact with hers.

> *Yes, you want her,*
> *Look at her, you know you do.*
> *It's possible she wants you, too,*
> *There's one way to ask her.*
> *You don't know why,*
> *But you're dyin' to try,*
> *You wanna kiss the girl.*

Hannah sat frozen in place. His face was so close to hers, she could feel his breath on her lips.

"Hannah," he breathed.

"Yeah?" she asked, feeling dizzy as her breathing came in quick spurts. Chace moved back a few inches.

"Can I kiss the girl?" he whispered softly. Unable to get a word out, Hannah nodded her answer to him.

Chace smiled, moving his hand up to cup her face. His thumbs made small circles on her skin as he gently pulled her face closer. His lips touched hers so lightly, at first, she didn't know if they had actually touched. Slowly his lips pressed down on hers and Hannah's world spun. She could not have imagined a sweeter kiss if she tried.

I'm dreaming, I have to be, her mind whirled. She kissed him back softly. Their lips intermingled together perfectly as if designed that way by God.

Slowly, Chace's lips parted with hers and she thought her heart was going to give out. He inched his face away, but his hands remained on her face. The look he gave her was so intense that Hannah felt she could see into his soul.

"You don't know how long I've been wanting to do that," he remarked, dropping his hands and clasping hers instead.

"I'm really glad you did, because I've wanted you to," Hannah smiled happily.

December 24th, 2018

The next morning Hannah woke up feeling like she was floating. She felt like she had been smiling in her sleep. Her tender moment with Chace the previous night played on loop in her head. She touched her lips, remembering the gentleness of his lips on hers.

Hannah's excitement doubled as she realized today was the day the ship docked at their first destination. It was also Christmas Eve. It felt strange looking out her small window and seeing the ocean and knowing it was almost Christmas.

Before departing the ship, Hannah had made plans to have breakfast with her group and they would talk about what plans they had for the day at Great Stirrup Cay. She was anxious to see what the Bahama's looked like up close and personal.

Hannah knocked on Kaylee and Aaron's door to see if they were ready. Aaron answered the door, his face drawn. She knew something was wrong. Aaron let her in and she went to Kaylee, who was lying under the covers in her bed.

"Kaylee, I'm worried about you," Hannah said, voicing her concern.

"Hannah, I'm just having stomach problems. It's nothing to worry about," she responded, sitting herself up.

"No, I'm not accepting that anymore. You need to see the doctor," proclaimed Hannah, sitting on the edge of the bed.

"I told her the same thing," said Aaron, picking up some discarded clothes on the floor.

"See, even your husband is telling you that," Hannah pointed out.

"You are both worry warts. It's like I've never been sick before," Kaylee commented, looking at Aaron and Hannah like they had lost their minds.

"Well, excuse us for being concerned," said Aaron flatly. Kaylee rolled her eyes.

"Kaylee, please just go see what the doctor has to say? For me?" begged Hannah. Kaylee thought for a moment and must have seen something in Hannah's eyes. She sighed, rubbing her eyes.

"Okay, okay. I will go. Aaron, will you come with me?" she asked, turning to her husband. Aaron looked relieved that she had finally agreed. He nodded his head and went to get dressed.

"Do you want me to come, too?" Hannah asked, helping Kaylee out of bed. Kaylee lightly swatted away her sister's offer.

"No, Hannah. I don't need both of you hovering over me when I talk to the doctor," she laughed. Hannah rolled her eyes.

"Honestly, Kaylee! You can be so stubborn," she declared, heading for the door. Kaylee giggled.

"But you wouldn't have me any other way," she smiled, winking at her sister. Hannah smiled. She was about to walk out when she remembered they were supposed to have breakfast together.

"I take it we aren't doing breakfast?" Hannah asked, already knowing the answer.

"That would be a no. Please let Hunter know that we won't be going. If Aaron and I decide to go to shore, why don't we meet at the Lighthouse Beach Bar around noon? I read that they have good drinks," suggested Kaylee.

"Okay, that works," Hannah agreed.

"But don't come looking for me if we don't show up. All that means is that I'm either too tired or not feeling up to it. If it's something serious, I'll send Aaron to meet you there at that time," Kaylee instructed, covering all the bases. Hannah sighed but agreed to go with her sister's plan.

She watched as Aaron and Kaylee walked down the hallway to the elevator. Then she remembered that Kaylee asked her to tell Hunter about breakfast. Hannah looked over at his cabin door.

Might as well get this over with, she

thought grudgingly.

~~*~*~*

Hunter felt a slight pounding in his head when he woke up. He knew he had a little too much to drink the previous night at the dance club. But watching Hannah's face while Chace sang hit him right where it hurt. He didn't know why it hurt so much. Yes, he liked Hannah, but it's not like they ever had something.

I guess I just wanted to be that person, he thought.

While he got ready for the day, thoughts swirled around in his head. Should he continue to try and pursue her? Could he accept just being friends as enough? Could he be okay seeing her with Chace? Hunter growled at the never-ending questions that consumed his thoughts.

A light knock at the door brought him out of his thought process. When he opened the door, he saw Hannah.

"Hannah. Hi," he spoke softly. He was surprised she was there, especially after how he had acted the other night.

"Hey, Hunter," she replied, looking down at the floor.

"Listen, about last night," he started before Hannah raised her hand to stop him.

"No, that's not why I'm here. I just wanted to let you know that Kaylee still isn't feeling well, and that her and Aaron went to see the doctor on board," she explained.

"Really? Oh man, I hope she's okay," said Hunter concerned. Hannah worried her lip and he could tell she was anxious about her sister.

"Hey, she'll be okay," he said, touching her shoulder to comfort her. To his surprise, she didn't shove him away. He thought about pulling her in for a hug but decided not to.

"Why don't we go get breakfast?" Hunter suggested, showing her a smile. Hannah looked up at him with uncertainty in her beautiful green eyes.

"I promise I won't bite," he joked, trying to lighten the mood. Hannah smiled a little bit and sighed.

"I don't know, Hunter," she hesitated.

"Come on, Hannah, it's just breakfast. We've had breakfast together for the past few days now," he pointed out.

"Yes, but my sister and Aaron were there, too," she remarked.

"Look, I'm sorry for last night. I won't force you to do anything you don't want to," said Hunter, almost ready to give up.

"Okay," Hannah agreed quietly. Hunter was almost positive he had imagined it. He smiled at her and went to put his shoes on.

As they walked down the hallway, Hunter stole a peak at Hannah. She was quiet but didn't seem to be nervous. He hoped this would be a good time to talk to her one on one.

Hunter chose to sit across the small table from Hannah. He had wanted to sit next to her, but he knew she might not have wanted that.

"So what do you have planned today? Are you going to explore Great Stirrup Cay?" he asked curiously. Hannah took a small bite of her bagel before she answered.

"Honestly, I'm not sure just yet. With Kaylee and Aaron not here to be a part of the planning, I don't know what I want to do," she answered.

"Why don't we go? I read they have a really great beach trail that would be nice to walk along," Hunter offered. Hannah pursed her lips looking down at her bagel.

"Can't we just hang out together as friends?" he inquired, starting to get frustrated.

Keep it cool, man, he thought to himself, taking a deep breath.

"Yes, we could hang out as friends, but I get the feeling that you want more than friendship," she stated.

"And what if I did? Would that be so horrible? Are you so nervous that you don't even want to be around me unless Kaylee and Aaron are around?" he asked confused.

"No, it's not that. I just don't know if I'm comfortable being alone with you when I know you have feelings for me," responded Hannah quietly. Anger burned in his stomach. He knew why she was saying this.

"Hannah, why can't *I* have an opportunity to get to know you? Is *he* the only one who gets that chance?" he asked, trying to keep the acid out of his tone.

Hannah looked at him wide eyed and he could see a blush creeping onto her face. She didn't answer him right away, but he could see that she was clearly flustered. She started picking away at her bagel depositing the pieces onto her plate. Hunter closed his eyes for a moment, trying to figure out a way to save this plummeting conversation. All he could think about was telling her the flat out truth.

"Hannah, I do like you. I won't lie. I do," Hunter blurted out. He could see her wince a little at his declaration.

"I don't mind being your friend," she commented, looking up at him tentatively.

"I guess that's all I can ask for at the moment," Hunter relented, feeling the fight blow out of him.

Hannah relaxed in her chair. He wanted to erase the whole conversation, but what was done was done. He would have to find a different approach to try and salvage any hope there was left. If there was any.

~~*~*~*

Chace sat eating breakfast with his friends, but he was having a hard time concentrating on the conversation they were having. He knew they were discussing what they wanted to do at Great Stirrup Cay, but all he could think about was Hannah.

The previous night he had put his heart on the line for her. When Chace saw the expression on her face as he sang to her, he knew his heart was gone. Hannah's beautiful eyes staring into his eyes was a feeling he had never experienced before. And the kiss he shared with her had sealed his fate. He felt like his heart belonged to her.

"Chace? Earth to Chace?" called a voice

next to him. Chace looked around and saw his three companions staring at him curiously.

"Sorry," he grimaced.

"Honestly, Chace, you're acting like a love sick puppy, Lana smiled, shaking her head. Chace sighed. He knew she was right.

"Why don't you ask her if she'd like to join us on the island today?" asked Jake, taking a large bight of his egg and cheese biscuit.

"I don't want to take away all her time from her family," he replied, knowing full well that he would love to spend every moment with Hannah if he could.

"Isn't that her over there?" Dan pointed. Chace glanced over his shoulder where Dan was looking. He saw Hannah's red curly hair flowing over the backrest of the chair she was in. And she wasn't alone. Hunter sat across the table from her.

"Isn't that the guy you mentioned the other night? The one that you think likes her?" asked Lana suspiciously.

Chace couldn't help but feel a twinge of betrayal at seeing the two of them eating breakfast alone. Hannah had told him she didn't feel comfortable being around Hunter alone.

"She looks a little distressed," Jake mentioned.

Chace took a closer look at the two. Hannah's head was facing down and she was picking her bagel to shreds. Hunter looked upset the way he was talking. He saw Hannah shrink back from something Hunter said. Chace stood up almost knocking the chair to the ground.

"Easy, Chace. Why don't I go talk to her?" suggested Lana, tugging on Chace's forearm. He looked down at Lana for a moment torn.

"I can tell she doesn't want to be there by her body language. Having you go barging in to "save the day" might not go over very well with the other guy, and I don't want to see a fight. So let me go talk to her and see if I can get her to come join us on the deck," Lana purposed.

What she said made sense, and it would be better not to cause a scene. He knew Hunter would want to start something, especially after the previous nights encounter.

"We can meet you right outside there, okay?" confirmed Lana, pointing to the deck outside the window.

"Come on, Chace. Let the woman do her thing," Jake smiled, patting him on the back. Jake and Dan got up and threw their trash away before heading outside.

"She saw me last night. She knows I'm part of your group. I think she'll come with me," said Lana, standing in front of him.

"Alright, I'll go outside," he agreed, giving in to Lana's plan. She smiled shooing him out. Chace looked over his shoulder at Hannah once more as he stepped outside to join his friends.

~~*~*~*

Hannah mulled around the confession Hunter had given her. Now, instead of just speculating, she knew that he did indeed like her. What he was saying about letting him have a chance would seem fair in any other situation. But she didn't want to reveal to him how strongly she felt about Chace. They agreed to be friends, but sitting there with him still felt awkward. Hannah tried to think of a way that she could end breakfast with him.

"Excuse me? I don't mean to interrupt anything, but is your name Hannah?" asked a female voice. Hannah looked up and recognized the raven haired woman from Chace's group the night before. What was she doing here?

"Yeah, I'm Hannah," she replied confused.

"Oh, good. My name is Lana. I've been asked to deliver a private message to you. Would you mind coming with me?" Lana asked smiling brightly. Hannah looked at Hunter. He was looking suspiciously at Lana.

"Uh, yeah. I'll come with you. Hunter, I'll see you later, okay?" said Hannah, getting up from the table. Hunter looked dejected that she was leaving so abruptly. He nodded his head and Hannah followed Lana out of the room to the deck.

"I know that wasn't the best formal introduction, but it's nice to meet you, Hannah. I am a friend of Chace," Lana smiled. Hannah smiled back. She liked this woman already.

"It's nice to meet you, too, Lana," she responded.

"I'm sure you're wondering what the "message" is that I needed to deliver. I hope you don't mind that I fibbed a little. See, Chace saw you sitting with your...friend?" Lana asked before continuing. Hannah shook her head to confirm.

"Hunter," Hannah replied.

"Yes, him. He saw you sitting with him and noticed you looked uncomfortable. He was about to come over their and confront Hunter on the situation, but I offered to rescue you instead," Lana explained proudly. Hannah's eyebrows rose. Lana faltered at her silence.

"You did seem like you weren't comfortable at the table. Did we read that wrong?" she asked.

"No, you were right. Sorry, I'm just surprised, that's all," Hannah smiled.

Lana returned her smile and motioned for Hannah to follow her. Turning a corner on the deck, Hannah saw Chace sitting with two other men. Her heart leaped into her throat as he looked up and smiled.

"Hannah," was all he said as he rose from his deck chair to meet her. He took her hand in his and led her away from his friends momentarily.

"Is everything okay?" he asked apprehensively.

"It is now. Lana is officially the heroine of the day," Hannah laughed lightly.

"Well, I'm glad she could get you. When I saw you sitting with Hunter I was confused, but then I noticed you seemed uncomfortable. I was ready to go over to you, but Lana thought it would be better if she went," said Chace.

"Yeah, she told me. My sister is not feeling well, so her and her husband went to the doctor to see if he could give her something. She had me tell Hunter that they wouldn't be there for breakfast. He asked if I'd eat with him and I figured that was harmless enough being in a public place. But he started talking about his feelings and it just got really awkward," Hannah explained. She rubbed her forehead in frustration.

"So he does like you," Chace responded in a cool tone. Hannah nodded. He lifted her chin gently so she was looking at him.

"And do you reciprocate his feelings toward you," he asked, catching her eye.

"No, I don't have feelings for him in that way. I told him I could be his friend, but hopefully he sees that that's all it will be," she answered. Chace sighed in relief.

"Well, let me introduce you to the rest of my group," he said, walking back to his friends. After meeting Chace's group, everyone thought it would be fun to hang out with Hannah as their fifth member. She was delighted that they wanted to include her. Their plan was that everyone would gather what they needed from their cabins and meet in the atrium by the Christmas tree.

Hannah quickly gathered her things for the beach remembering not to forget the sunscreen. With her pale skin, a sun burn was inevitable if she didn't protect herself. Packing a few more items, Hannah was ready to go.

By the time she made it down to the Christmas tree, Chace and his friends were already there. Excitement rose within her as they walked down the gangway to the island.

The weather was warm and balmy, but a

light breeze made it almost perfect. The sun felt so good on Hannah's face. As she gazed out at the beautiful island, the first thing that caught her attention was the white, sandy beach and the amazing crystal clear blue-green water lapping peacefully onto shore.

Hundreds of blue beach chairs lined the beach just begging for someone to claim a spot on the tranquil sand.

"Oh my gosh! Guys, we have to go to the beach first! It's too beautiful to pass up!" exclaimed Lana excitedly. Hannah secretly agreed. She couldn't wait to get her toes into the warm sand.

Many passengers from the ship were already on the island and chair space was limited. But they managed to find some chairs that were next to each other toward the right side of the coastline.

"Jake, can you help me get some sunscreen on my back, please?" Lana asked, handing her husband the sunscreen bottle. He happily obliged and spread the white cream along her back.

Hannah fluffed her turquoise towel out onto her chair. After removing her shirt, and shorts, she began to apply her own sunscreen. She loved the dark blue bathing suit she had bought for the trip. It was a high neck halter top that crisscrossed in the back with a standard bikini bottom of the same color.

She tried to get as much of her back as she could, but it was hard to get in between the bathing suit straps where they crossed on her upper back. She was about to let it go and pray that none of the skin between the strings wouldn't get burnt.

"Would it be okay if I helped you get that area on your back?" asked Chace.

Hannah saw him standing beside her in his dark red swim shorts. Her eyes scaled up his defined stomach and lean chest muscles as her breath caught in her throat. She tried not to stare as a blush crept onto her cheeks.

"Yeah, that would be great. I really don't want to have to deal with a sunburn on my first day off the ship," she commented, handing Chace the bottle. She pulled her hair up into a messy bun so that the lotion wouldn't get in her hair.

Squeezing some sunscreen into his hands, he turned to apply it to Hannah's back. The feeling of his hands on her back did crazy things to her stomach. His hands were gentle as he moved the strings out of the way to get what she couldn't.

"There we go. I think you're set," Chace announced, closing the lid to the sunscreen.

"Chace, let's go see if we can rent some body boards," Jake suggested. Chace and Dan both went with Jake to the small shack that advertised rentals.

"Do you ladies want to try?" Dan asked, when they returned. All three guys had body boards in their hands. Jake looked like he was itching to get to the water.

"No, I'm good. I'll meet you guys out there in a few," Lana answered, laying on her stomach on one of the chairs. Her hair had been pulled up with a large clip and she rested her head sideways on her arms.

The guys looked at Hannah with the same question on their faces. She had never been on a surf board, let alone a small body board, and she wasn't sure if she wanted to test her balance out on the water yet.

"I'll stay with Lana for a bit," she responded, smiling at Chace. All three men exchanged looks before racing to the water's edge.

"They're like a bunch of kids," Lana laughed, propping her chin on her arms. Hannah giggled, looking out as Jake slid his body board on the water and ran after it. He jumped onto the board and held out for a second before falling backward onto the wet sand.

She watched as Chace gave it a go. He tossed the board on the water and caught up to it quickly. Once he made it on the board, he surfed the water's edge for about three seconds before falling off into the shallow water. She smiled as he waved to her.

"You know he's absolutely taken by you," Lana remarked. Hannah glanced over at her, her eyebrows raising at her statement. Lana laughed and turned on her side facing Hannah.

"Don't look so shocked. I've never seen him look at a woman the way he looks at you. Of course I didn't know him before he moved to Tennessee, but even with his ex girlfriend, Lacy, he never looked at her that way," Lana commented, smiling at her.

Hannah looked out at Chace again. They had moved deeper into the water trying to catch some small waves. She couldn't help but feel excitement at what Lana had said. She knew that Chace had feelings for her because of the song he had sung to her and the sweet kiss they had shared the previous night. But to hear it from his friend made it even more real.

"And I can't help but notice the way your eyes light up when you look at him. You really like him, don't you?" asked Lana boldly.

"Yes, I do like him...a lot," she admitted, pursing her lips as she smiled.

"Has he kissed you yet?" Lana asked, a mischievous smile dancing on her lips. Hannah laughed lightly.

"Last night," she answered, remembering the feeling of electricity flowing through her body when his lips touched hers. Lana's smile grew wider.

"You're good for him. I can see so much more life in him since he's met you," said Lana, sitting up. Hannah beamed at her statement.

"Okay, enough lovey-dovey talk. Let's get into that water!" declared Lana. Hannah nodded in agreement as they went out to join the rest of their party.

~~*~*~*

Chace had never been to a tropical island before, but he didn't think it could have been anything like this. There he was with the closest friends he had, enjoying the most beautiful beach he had ever seen. And on top of all that, he was with Hannah.

Chace watched as she and Lana waded in the water, letting the waves lap up against their knees. She was talking animatedly with Lana about something and he could tell that they were becoming good friends. He had felt bad for Lana because she had to go on a cruise with a bunch of guys. But now that Hannah was there, Lana seemed to appreciate a female companion.

Hannah laughed at something Lana had said and an intense feeling welled up in his heart. She was perfect in every way he could imagine. He knew he was losing himself to her quickly. She looked flawless in her deep blue bathing suit. Jake had slapped him in the back of the head lightly when Hannah was putting sunscreen on because Chace was noticeably staring.

As time went on, the group went back to their beach chairs. Checking his phone, Chace saw that it was around ten-thirty. No one had anything planned after the beach and he wanted to spend some time with Hannah.

"Hannah I was wondering if you would like to walk along the beach path they have here," he suggested, putting on a white shirt. Hannah had put on a short white sun dress over her bathing suit and she had let her hair down. A true vision of beauty.

"Yeah, that would be fun," she smiled, slipping on her sandals.

"What are you guys going to be doing?" Chace asked, looking over to his friends.

"Jake, Dan and I are going to go kayaking," Lana answered, packing her towel in her beach bag.

"Well, do you want to meet up for lunch?"

Chace inquired.

"We probably won't be back in time for lunch. We are doing the Kayak tour so that will probably be a while. We'll meet you guys back on the ship," Jake replied, dusting white sand off of his legs.

The group split up and went their separate ways. Chace and Hannah found some lockers to store their belongings in while they went on their walk. The water looked so clear as they walked on the soft dirt path. Chace looked down at Hannah and saw that she was looking at the ground with a concerned look on her face.

"Penny for your thoughts," he said, nudging Hannah in the arm.

"Hmm? Oh! I'm sorry, Chace. I guess I got caught up in my thoughts about my sister," she said as she bit her lower lip.

"What's wrong with Kaylee?" he asked, as the path started to veer further away from the beach. Long, tall grass-like plants grew on either side of the trail.

"She hasn't been feeling well. I finally convinced her to go talk to the doctor on the ship with Aaron," she answered, looking out on the trail in front of them.

"Hey, I'm sure she will be okay. Do you want to go back to the ship and see if she knows anything?" Chace asked. Hannah stopped and looked up at him with such turmoil that his heart went out to her. She offered a small smile.

"Thank you, but we told each other that we would meet at the Lighthouse Beach Bar at noon. She said if everything was fine then her and Aaron would both be there. If she was feeling sick and didn't want to come to shore, she would send Aaron to tell me it was nothing serious. So either way I'll find out, but I have to be there," she explained.

"We can do that. I'll make sure we don't miss the time," he assured her. Hannah still seemed bugged about something. Chace took her hand and guided her over to a bench shaded by the tall grass.

"Something is still wrong," he observed as they sat down. Hannah was quiet for a few moments before she responded. Her focus went to the ground again.

"Kaylee is all I have. Ever since my mom died and my dad ran off, all I've ever had was Kaylee. So when she gets sick I always become this anxious woman who suddenly feels like a fourteen year old girl again.

"When I was sixteen years old I remember making plans with some of my friends months in advance to go to a concert. Kaylee had come down with a bad cold and Aaron was visiting his parents out of state for the weekend. I was so scared of her being sick that I canceled the concert and stayed with her. She begged me to go, telling me that it was just "some snot and a headache" and that she didn't need my help. She ended up being fine. I just fear losing her," said Hannah, her voice breaking on the last word.

A tear rolled down her cheek and Chace wiped it away with his finger. He couldn't imagine what it would be like to have nowhere to go should a situation arise. She had a lot of strength in her character, but he could tell she was also as fragile as a butterfly wing.

"I have a good feeling she will be okay. Just hang in there, okay?" he encouraged, wrapping his arm around her shoulders. Hannah leaned into him and sighed.

"I know you're right. Kaylee calls me a worry wart," she laughed lightly. Chace smiled, rubbing his thumb on her arm. She looked up at him and smiled brightly.

"Thanks," she whispered, her green eyes shimmering from unshed tears.

Hannah parted her lips and her gaze shifted to his mouth. Before he knew what was happening, Hannah closed the gap between them and pressed her perfect pink lips onto his. Shock radiated through him as her lips moved softly with his. Kissing Hannah was the most exhilarating feeling Chace had ever experienced.

~~*~*~*

Hannah could not believe how bold she was being. She kissed him after only having him kiss her once. She was never the type of person to make a move on a guy. But his lips meshed perfectly with hers and she was lost in her own personal paradise, her heart beating furiously.

"Do you thank everyone this way?" he whispered on her lips. Hannah could feel his smile on her lips as a blushed crept onto her face.

"I'm sorry. I'm usually not so daring," she admitted as they pulled away from one another.

Chace chuckled, moving a piece of her hair behind her ear.

"I hope you're not sorry," he responded.

"I didn't mean I was sorry for kissing you," Hannah smirked, standing up.

"Good, because I'm not sorry you did," he said, reaching for her hand. Hannah accepted it happily and they started walking back toward the beach.

As they arrived at the Lighthouse Beach Bar, Hannah searched for Kaylee or Aaron, trying not to panic as her thoughts whirled around frantically.

"I see your sister," announced Chace, pointing to one of the picnic benches by the bar. Hannah saw both Kaylee and Aaron and immediately her swirling thoughts subsided. They were both their which meant Kaylee was feeling well enough to come to shore.

"Kaylee! How are you feeling? What did the doctor say? Did he have any answers for you?" she blurted out, sitting across the table from the two. Chace sat down next to her.

"Hannah, I'm fine! Nothing is wrong with me. The doctor assured us that I have nothing to worry about. But he did have a message for you," she commented, smiling widely. Hannah looked at her sister confused.

"For *me*?"

"Yes. He told me to tell you to make sure you don't injure your wrist anymore or you won't be able to hold the baby," Kaylee remarked, smiling ear to ear.

Hannah looked back and forth between Kaylee and Aaron. Both had the same slap happy look on their faces. She glanced over at Chace to see that his eyebrows were raised and he was smiling.

Okay, what am I not getting here? I won't be able to hold the baby if I hurt my wrist. What baby? Who's having a... Hannah thought to herself before the light clicked on. Her eyes grew wide and she began to scream. She jumped up from the table and ran around to her sister.

"Kaylee, are you pregnant?" she shrieked. Kaylee's red hair bobbed up and down as she nodded her head.

"Oh my gosh! I can't believe it! I'm going to be an Aunt! You're going to be a mommy!" Hannah gushed, tears streaming down her face. She hugged Kaylee and Aaron tightly.

"Congrats, you guys," Chace voiced, extending his hand to Aaron. Aaron smiled proudly and shook his hand. Kaylee, smiling with tears in her eyes, looked over to Chace and thanked him.

"This is crazy! What an awesome Christmas gift!" Hannah exclaimed happily.

The rest of the day passed in a blur for Hannah. After having lunch with Chace, Kaylee and Aaron the group spent the rest of the afternoon exploring the small island, eventually making their way back to the ship.

With all of the emotions Hannah had dealt with that day, she felt exhausted by dinner time.

"Hannah, you look beat," Kaylee mentioned as the group finished their dinner. The four had chosen to eat at the Cucina del Capitano. Hannah had been excited to have

Chace join them. He seemed to fit in well with them and that gave her a warm, fuzzy feelings.

"I am pretty tired, but more emotionally then physically. But I need to do a few things before tomorrow," Hannah mentioned, wiping her mouth on a napkin.

"Well, I know it's only around six o'clock, but you're not the only one who's drained," Kaylee exclaimed, hiding a yawn. Hannah smiled widely.

"I still can't believe you're pregnant, Kaylee!" she gushed.

"I know. It all seems so surreal," said Kaylee, glancing at Aaron. He smiled lovingly at her as he kissed her forehead.

"Do you want to head back to the cabin? Or was there something else you wanted to do before turning in?" Kaylee asked her husband.

"Actually, I will meet you there. It won't be long," Aaron responded. Kaylee nodded and said her goodbye's. Aaron turned to Hannah and Chace.

"I want to browse some gift shops to see if I can find something special for Kaylee for Christmas tomorrow," he announced.

"It was fun hanging out with you, Chace," he added.

"Likewise. Oh, and congrats again on the baby," he answered. Aaron nodded his head in gratitude and went on his way.

"I should probably check in with my friends to see what their plans are for tomorrow before it gets too late," said Chace, checking the time. Hannah tried to hide her disappointment of seeing him go. He looked over toward her and smiled, taking her hand.

"Will you meet me at the Christmas tree in the atrium around nine tonight?" he asked.

"Yeah, I'd love that," she responded smiling. Chace kissed her hand and walked off in the same direction Aaron had just gone, leaving Hannah staring after him in a daze.

~~*~*~*

Chace smiled to himself as he headed for deck five. He had told Hannah he was going to see his friends, but only to throw her off from his real plan. He had wanted to get a moment to himself so he could find Hannah a Christmas gift.

Entering the first gift shop, Chace heard twinkly Christmas music playing. Looking around, he noticed souvenirs of the cruise line from magnets to sweatshirts. There were beach themed areas that had bottles of sand and shells in them, and small rhinestone flip flips dangling from a necklace.

Deciding that wasn't the shop he was looking for, Chace headed to the shop next door. It was a little fancier with jewelry and other high end items. He was about to walk back out, but decided to give it a try. He didn't want to overwhelm Hannah by getting her something flashy, but he did want to get her something nice.

Gazing through the plate glass at all the beautiful items, Chace thought about how much Hannah had come to mean to him. This was just his third day knowing her and already his heart was taken. He didn't think feelings like this were possible so early on. She wasn't even his girlfriend and here he was buying her a Christmas present.

Strolling to the end of one of the glass cases, he found some colorful necklaces. His attention was drawn to a necklace with a beautiful turquoise blue stone as thick as his thumb and an inch and a half in length. Sterling silver enclosed the gem in the shape of an oval as two silver vines wrapped around the front of the blue crystal. At the top of the of the pendant was a small diamond secured near the hook where the chain met the jewelry.

Chace looked at that necklace for a long time. Something about it screamed Hannah. Could he buy something like that for her? Would she think it was too much?

"Hello there! May I help you with something?" asked a tall blond woman behind the counter. Chace pursed his lips and nodded his head.

"Yeah, I would like to see that turquoise oval necklace, please?" he asked politely.

"Ah, the Diamond Rock Crystal. An excellent choice!" she exclaimed as she opened the cabinet with one of her many keys and presented the necklace to him. Chace studied the multifaceted crystal and how the light bounced off of it.

"Hmm, let's see. You care a lot about her, but you're timid about your feelings for her," observed the jewelry consultant. Chace looked up at her awestruck.

How could she possibly know that? he

thought in amazement. The blond smiled with a knowing look.

"I can see it in your eyes. I think this would be the perfect gift. It is simple, yet elegant and beautiful," she explained.

"How much is it?" he asked, looking for a price.

She flipped the necklace over and looked at the tiny tag, adjusting her glasses.

"It is $240.00, but for you and your special lady, I will go to $220.00," she responded, giving Chace a wink. He thought for a moment, knowing the deal was a bargain for such a beautiful piece of jewelry.

"I'll do it," Chace agreed. He followed the sales woman to the checkout counter and completed the transaction. She gave him a red velvet box with a green bow wrapped around it.

"Merry Christmas," she smiled as he left the gift shop with his prize.

~~*~*~*

(Earlier that day)

Hunter had spent the morning in a mindless fog. When Hannah had left him at breakfast with the woman who claimed to have a message for her, he sat at the table for a while wallowing in self pity. He just couldn't understand why Hannah wasn't letting him in.

He decided to go ashore to see if there was anything interesting to do, and see if he could spot Hannah. Around noon, he ventured over to the Lighthouse Beach Bar to grab a bite to eat. He was surprised to see Aaron and

Kaylee sitting there.

"Aaron, Kaylee, what's up?" Hunter asked, sitting down across from them. Both turned their attention to him and smiled.

"Hey, Hunter! You'll never believe what we found out this morning!" exclaimed Kaylee, glancing excitedly at Aaron.

"Well, spill it! What did you find out?" Hunter wanted to know.

"Kaylee's pregnant!" Aaron announced. Hunter sat dumbfounded for a moment. His long time best friend was going to be a father. Why did that rub him the wrong way? He should be happy for the couple. They deserved all the happiness in the world.

"It's about time!" Hunter declared, faking his enthusiasm. He didn't want to ruin the moment with his take on the news. Kaylee smiled from ear to ear, clearly overjoyed.

"I'm really happy for you guys. A baby is huge news! Is that why you've been sick?" he asked. Kaylee nodded in response.

"Well, I'm going to buy you a beer, my man," Hunter insisted, shifting his attention to Aaron.

"Thanks, Hunter. I actually just had a couple at lunch. Mind if I catch a rain check on that for tonight?" Aaron inquired.

"Oh, yeah. That sounds good to me. But I'm going to head over to the bar and get one for myself," he stated, walking over to the bar.

As he paid for his beer, Hunter noticed something red in his peripheral. Glancing over he saw Hannah was walking toward the bar. His excitement over seeing her quickly diminished when he saw Chace by her side holding her hand. As much as he wanted to see her, having an encounter with Chace was not something he was up for. He decided it was his time to make an exit.

"I think I'm going to go check out the waves," Hunter claimed, making his way back to Aaron and Kaylee.

"That sounds fun. I know we want to make it over to the beach sometime today. Maybe we'll see you there," replied Kaylee, smiling brightly at him.

"Sounds great! Hope to catch you guys there," Hunter responded.

"We'll see you later," Aaron answered. Hunter smiled and quickly walked off in the direction of the beach. Turning around yards away, he saw Hannah and Chace approaching Kaylee and Aaron. He blew out a sigh of relief that he had dodged that rendezvous.

Once back on the ship later on that day, Hunter came across a flower shop. Wandering inside, he was bombarded with the mixed aromas of all the flowers. There were red, pink and yellow roses, and wild arrangements of tropical flowers. Hunter stopped in front of a single red rose in a small vase with baby's breath surrounding the delicate flower. Picking up the vase, he walked over to the counter and made his purchase.

Now to find Hannah, he thought, exiting the flower shop.

~~*~*~*

Hannah put the final touches to her hair that she had been working on for thirty minutes. She wanted to put a wave to her hair. By the time she finished her hair she had to take a breath.

Now I remember why I don't like doing my own hair, she thought with a huff. But looking in the mirror she knew her efforts were worth it. Her hair looked great and came out just as she wanted it to.

Kaylee may be the hair stylist, but I don't do too bad myself, she giggled to herself.

Checking herself over once more, Hannah made sure everything looked good. She could feel that tonight was going to be memorable. Her dark red dress came down to the middle of her thigh, and the long sleeves had a slit going the up the arms, revealing her freckled skin. Lastly, she chose a pair of white lace knee high heels that hugged her legs.

Hannah smiled at her reflection. She grabbed a small bag of items she had bought for Chace that she wanted to give to him that night. She knew it was only Christmas Eve, but she felt like it was the right time while they were sitting by the Christmas tree all lit up.

Hannah checked the clock and saw that it was eight thirty. Normally she would have waited, but tonight she wanted to go early. She wanted to sit by the tree and be able to look at its festive decorations a bit before Chace came.

Hannah felt a light spring to her step as she walked to the elevator and made her way to the atrium. As she exited the elevator, Hannah's breath caught at the sight of the exquisite Christmas tree in front of her. She hadn't seen the tree during the evening and she was blown away at how it illuminated the entire room.

She sat herself down on one of the couches surrounding the magnificent tree, setting her gifts for Chace on the floor by her feet. Hannah was surprised that there weren't any people there.

I could sit in front of this tree for hours! she thought, gazing at all the decorations strewn perfectly on the tree. It looked just like a picture out of a fancy Christmas magazine.

Hannah heard footsteps behind her and smiled, anxious to see Chace again. But when she turned around it was not Chace's face she saw. She was looking up at Hunter. He was holding a small vase with a red rose in it. He gave her a sheepish grin and came around to sit by her on the couch.

"How did you know that I was going to be here?" Hannah questioned him.

"Honestly, I didn't. I was on my way up to your cabin to see you, but when I was in the elevator, I saw you sitting here," Hunter explained. Hannah looked at the rose in his hands. Hunter followed her gaze.

"I bought this for you. Merry Christmas," he stated softly as he handed her the small vase. Hannah couldn't help but smile. She loved roses and she knew it was a sweet gesture.

"Thank you, Hunter. It's really pretty," she commented, smelling the rose. Hunter grinned and moved a little closer to her.

"Hannah, I need to talk to you. Please hear me out?" he asked, his eyes beseeching hers. Hannah drew in a deep breath.

"Okay," she responded cautiously, fiddling with the hem of her dress.

"Okay, I need you to know that I care about you. I know we haven't spent much time together, but I do have feelings for you. I hadn't noticed you before at your sister's wedding, but man I should have paid closer attention. You are such a beautiful woman and I am taken by your gentle smile and captivating eyes.

"I am a good guy and I would treat you with respect. If you wanted to take things slowly I would wait as long as you wanted. Will you let me have the opportunity to show you what I have to give?" Hunter asked quietly. She didn't know what to say. Her heart was pounding and her mouth went dry.

Why, oh why is this happening!? her conscience screamed.

"Hunter, I..." she began, seeking out the right words to say.

Hannah stood up and paced in front of him, chewing her lip. Hunter rose up and blocked her path. She collided with him and bounced backward. He caught her by the arms and steadied her.

"Why won't you let me in?" he whispered.

Hannah looked up and realized they were within inches from each other. She froze as his eyes locked onto hers. Inwardly, she was anything but calm. Voices hollered at her to step away, that something bad was about to happen.

Before she could react, Hunter brought

his head down to hers and kissed her. His kiss was soft and warm, his breath smelling of mint. But the kiss soon turned more urgent as he tried to get more of a response from her lips. Hannah's brain kicked into high gear and she shoved herself away from Hunter's grasp.

"You shouldn't have done that, Hunter," she stated angrily, creating more space between them. He looked disappointed by her rejection.

"Hannah, I'm sorry. I don't know what came over me," he exclaimed, frustrated over his actions getting the better of him again. He scowled at the floor.

"I think you need to go," Hannah suggested, crossing her arms. Hunter's head whipped up as his eyes grew wide in disbelief. Then, as if all the fight had left him, he hung his head in defeat. Without another word Hunter walked away, leaving her to her thoughts.

Hannah sat down on the couch again, but this time unable to enjoy the wonder of the Christmas tree. Hunter's kiss burned on her lips, but it was not in a way she enjoyed.

Why did he do that? she thought in frustration.

Time went by and eventually Hannah started to cool down. She wanted more than anything to run to Kaylee and tell her what happened, but she knew Chace was going to be there soon. She looked at the clock hanging up in the atrium. Chace was forty-five minutes late. Anxiety seized her. Had he stood her up?

Not Chace. He wouldn't do that...would he? Questions swirled in her head as she continued to wait.

Hannah lingered at the tree another fifteen minutes before she realized that Chace wasn't coming. A stabbing pain ruptured in her heart. Tears stung her eyes as she got up retrieving the rose Hunter had given her and Chace's gifts. Her feet felt heavy as she made her way to her sister's cabin. She knocked on the door and prayed that Kaylee was awake.

"Hannah? What's wrong?" asked Kaylee as she opened the door. Immediately, Hannah's tears were unleashed. She freed her hands and flung her arms around her sister.

"Hey, hey, it's okay. Come here. Tell me what happened," soothed Kaylee, bringing her over to the couch. Hannah looked around for Aaron. She heard the faint sound of the shower and figured that's where he was.

"He stood me up," was all she could get out before another round of tears made their way down her reddened cheeks.

"He *what*!?" Kaylee demanded. Hannah nodded her head yes, trying to get herself under control.

"I waited for an hour and he didn't show up," she explained, grabbing a tissue.

"Well, then who is the rose from?" Kaylee questioned, pointing to the vase.

"That would be from Hunter. He gave that to me before kissing me," she answered sniffling. Kaylee's eyes looked as though they would pop out of her head.

"Hunter *kissed* you!?" she asked perplexed. Hannah only nodded her head. She quickly recapped what happened.

"Wow...what a night *you've* had," Kaylee stated, blowing out an exaggerated sigh.

"What do I do about Chace, Kaylee?" she sniffled.

"You need to go ask him why he did that before I do," she responded, playfully puffing up her chest. Hannah giggled, hugging her sister.

"What about Hunter? It's going to be really awkward whenever we all hang out now," wondered Hannah.

"Don't worry about Hunter," Kaylee answered, walking Hannah to the door. She picked up her gifts to Chace. Kaylee hugged her tight and kissed her cheek.

Hannah pushed the button on the elevator for Chace's floor, fidgeting with the handle of the gift bags. She headed for his cabin, thankful that he had told her the number. Her heart raced as she reached out to knock on his door. Would he even be there? Her question was answered as the doorknob started to jiggle.

~~*~*~*

(Earlier that evening)

Chace put on his nicest black button up shirt and some tan pants. He was nervous about meeting up with Hannah, and he knew it was because he had bought her the necklace.

She'll like it. I know that. I just don't want her to feel pressured or anything, he told himself.

Chace headed down to the atrium. In the elevator, he observed the gigantic Christmas tree with all of its holiday trinkets hanging from the branches. Looking down, he could see Hannah sitting on the couch, but she wasn't alone. It looked like Hunter was sitting with her, but he couldn't get a good view.

Chace stepped out of the elevator and walked around the information desk. Hannah's back was to him but he confirmed that the man sitting with her was Hunter. Chace couldn't make out what they were saying, but he didn't want risk going closer just yet.

Hannah got up from the couch and started to pace back and forth in front of the tree. Chace chuckled. He had seen her do that before when she needed to work out her thoughts. But his chuckling stopped when Hunter stood up and blocked Hannah from her path, causing her to sway backward. He watched as Hunter caught her, holding her arms to steady her balance.

Hunter whispered something to Hannah that made her look up. He could feel the hair on the back of his neck raise at how close Hunter was to Hannah, but his heart stopped dead in its tracks when he saw Hunter bend down and kiss her.

Chace's heart sputtered. She didn't stop him or move away. He didn't understand. All this time she was saying she was uncomfortable around him, that she didn't want to be alone with him. But here she was kissing him.

Chace couldn't watch anymore. He trudged back to his cabin in a daze. When he reached his room, he fumbled with the key card to open his door.

"Chace, you alright?" asked a voice behind him. It was Jake. Chace turned to his friend and sighed.

"I saw Hannah kissing Hunter," he replied sullenly.

"Woah...that's rough. Here, let's go in and open a beer," advised Jake, taking Chace's room key and opening the door. Chace walked in, taking Hannah's gift out of his pocket and tossing it on the small table.

Guess I'll have to return that, he thought, a pain piercing his heart.

"Okay, start from the beginning," Jake instructed, handing him an opened beer. Chace explained the event he witnessed just moments before.

"It sounds like Hunter is the one that kissed her," Jake corrected when Chace finished his story. Chace downed his beer.

"Yes, but she didn't push away. And how did he know she was going to be there at that time? Did they plan to meet up at that same place before she met up with me?" he asked to no one in particular.

"Okay, before you start going down that road, I think you need to talk to Hannah. Get her side of the story," Jake suggested. Chace got up and opened another beer for himself.

"What's there to tell? That she *forgot* she could push him away? Or that she didn't *mean* to let him kiss her?" he sneered. Jake took the bottle of beer away from Chace.

"Listen, I don't think this is a good time for you to get wasted. Go see her," coaxed Jake, putting Chace's second beer back in the mini fridge.

"I don't know if I can do that right now," he replied, holding his head in his hands.

"Well, at least think about it. Hannah's a good girl. She's not Lacy. Don't jump to any rash conclusions until you talk to her," instructed Jake, heading for the door. Chace nodded as Jake left the room.

He knew Hannah wasn't like Lacy. Not in any way, shape or form. Hannah wasn't a lying, manipulative female who only wanted to be with him so he could buy her things. She was different, or so he had thought.

Chace retrieved the beer that Jake had put away. He told himself he would only have that one and then he would be done. He didn't like being drunk and Jake was right in the sense that it wasn't a good time to get wasted.

So many thoughts whizzed through his mind. After he finished his beer, he went over to his bed to lay down. He was anything but tired, but his head was starting to hurt. Images of Hannah in the arms of Hunter made his stomach nauseas, but they wouldn't leave his mind.

Chace tried to replay in his head what was going on before the kiss happened. He remembered Hannah pacing. At the time he had thought it was cute, but putting it together now he knew she was actually upset. Was Hunter pressuring her to do something?

Thoughts and questions bounced back and forth in Chace's head for the next hour. He had worn himself ragged with all the thinking he had been doing. He was tossing around the idea of whether or not he should go see Hannah or just call it a night and sleep on it. But his thoughts were interrupted when a knock sounded at the door.

Forcing himself up, Chace walked over to the door and squinted to see through the peephole. Shock rippled through him when he saw Hannah standing on the other side of his door. Animosity burned in his eyes and he was about to ignore her, but looking closer he could see that she had been crying....a lot. Her nose was Rudolph red, and her eyes looked puffy. He also noticed she was holding a small paper bag. Sighing deeply, Chace decided to open the door.

Here goes nothing, he thought.

Hannah's eyes went wide at seeing him. At first he registered hurt on her beautiful face, but that soon turned to agitation. They stood there at an awkward stand still, Hannah in the hall and Chace in the doorway. Hannah broke the silence.

"Why didn't you come? I waited over an hour for you," said she, her voice soft. The look in her eyes and the sound of her voice were contrasting each other and Chace couldn't figure out if she was sad or angry. Astonished that *she* could have any reason to be mad caused anger to flare inside of him.

"It didn't seem like you were lonely," he retorted, crossing his arms over his chest. Hannah looked at him puzzled.

"What does *that* mean?" she demanded. Chace's narrowed his eyes.

"It means that it looked like Hunter was keeping you plenty entertained when I came down," he spat.

Hannah looked as if she had been slapped in the face. Her cheeks grew red and her eyes welled up with tears.

"Chace, it's not what you think at all," she stated, two tears falling down her rosy cheeks. Something inside him urged him to hear her out. That something, or someone, sounded like Jake.

"Alright, come on in," Chace exhaled.

Hannah nodded and walked past him. He caught the scent of her perfume and almost groaned. She smelled so good. Closing the door behind him, he turned to her. For the first time he took notice of what she was wearing, especially her white lace boots.

How can I be mad at her when she's so damn beautiful, he thought.

"Here, come sit down," he instructed toward the couch.

Chace handed her a tissue before sitting down next to her. He tried not to sit too close even though that was all he wanted to do. He felt that he needed to keep his guard up in case the truth was bad.

"Why were you with Hunter?" he asked, needing to know the truth. Hannah shook her head.

"Hunter said he saw me in the elevator as he was going up. He had a rose in his hand and said he was going to go to my cabin," she started, a shiver emanating from her small frame. Was that discomfort he saw? His blood boiled at the thought of Hunter being in her room.

"But he said he saw me by the tree and went back down the elevator to me. He gave me the rose and asked if I would hear him out. I agreed. Hunter told me that he cared about me and had feelings for me. He was saying that he would treat me respectfully and that he would be patient," said Hannah, retelling the story.

"After he told me about his feelings. I got up and started to pace. He stood in my pacing path and almost knocked me over. After steadying me, he asked why I wouldn't let him in. And before I could answer him, he kissed me," she concluded. Chace was satisfied that she had told the truth, at least about what he had seen. Now came the hard part.

"Did you kiss him back?" he probed, almost wincing. Hannah shook her head.

"No. I was so frozen with shock that it took me a moment to register what was going on. I could hear myself thinking, "Stop, pull away!" but my body was slow to respond. When I did realize what was happening, I moved away from him and told him he shouldn't have done that and that he should leave," she finalized.

"I didn't see that last part. When Hunter kissed you, I couldn't take it, so I turned and left and I've been up here ever since," Chace explained.

"Well, that explains why you didn't show up," she said, looking down at her hands.

Now it was Chace's face that flushed. He thought about how she must have felt waiting there for him for an hour. She must have thought him a real jerk.

"Listen, you know that the only reason I

didn't come was because of what I saw. It really messed with me when I saw him kiss you," Chace admitted. He knew that he could believe Hannah and felt stupid for doubting her.

"No, I understand. If it had been the other way around and I saw another girl kissing you I probably would have done the same thing," she admitted, a small smile forming on her lips. Chace wet a tissue with some water and wiped a mascara trail off her cheek.

"I must look like a train wreck. At one point tonight I looked pretty good," she said, walking over to the mirror. Chace watched her fix her eyes the best she could before giving up and rejoining him on the couch.

"I still think you're beautiful," he remarked, cracking a half smile. Hannah blushed, nibbling on her lower lip. Chace refrained himself from attacking her with a kiss.

"Hey, I got something for you," he said, going to the table to retrieve her gift.

"Chace, you didn't have to get me anything," Hannah smiled, looking at the red velvet box, stroking the green bow.

"Well, I guess I can't say much because I got you something, too," she announced, presenting the gift bag to him.

"Open mine first," Hannah insisted, handing him the first of two small boxes from the bag.

Chace smiled and opened the lid. Inside, he saw a thin leather bracelet with a small wire hand connecting the bracelet together. He took the bracelet out and studied it for a moment.

Glancing at Hannah, her lips pursed together, he knew it had to mean something.

Finally, unable to guess, he looked up at her sheepishly, making her laugh. She stuck her right hand up wiggling her fingers. Chace chuckled when he put the pieces together.

"From when we first met," Hannah beamed.

"Yes, I remember now. That was a good day," he responded, remembering how cute she looked when she couldn't figure out how to wrap her sprained wrist. Hannah giggled, handing him the second gift.

"Why did you get me two?" he asked quizzically.

"Well, the first gift was more of a light-hearted laugh gift. This one has a little more meaning," she explained, her cheeks blushing.

Chace opened the box and saw a small flat silver fish tail hanging from a brown leather band. Pulling it all the way out, he noticed that it was a necklace. He turned it around and saw the inscription:

Kiss The Girl
~H~

It was then that Chace realized it wasn't a fish tail, but a mermaid tail. He liked the fact that it was a mans type of necklace, even though it was a mermaid tail. But his favorite feature was the *H* engraved on the back with the title of the song he had sung for her at the dance club.

"Do you like it?" she asked.

"I love it, actually. You're very good at gift giving," Chace complimented, slipping the necklace over his head. It rested perfectly below the base of his neck. Hannah smiled, clapping her hands in excitement.

"Your turn," he said, pointing to the red box next to her lap. Hannah gently removed the green bow. Chace held his breath as she opened the box. He watched as her eyes grew wide and her jaw fell slack.

"Chace...this is so beautiful," she spoke, studying it closer. Her doe eyes locked with his and he could see that she loved it.

"Here, let's put it on and see how it looks," he suggested, clasping the necklace around her neck. It hung gracefully on her upper chest and the little diamond sparkled with each breath she took. Hannah went to look in the mirror and then turned back to him with a smile on her lips.

"This is the most gorgeous Christmas present anyone has ever given me," she stated, sitting back down on the couch. Chace pulled her close to him and softly caressed her face with his thumb.

"I would not wish any companion in the world but you," Chace whispered in her ear. He could feel her shiver.

"Shakespeare?" she asked, letting out a small laugh. Chace nodded and smiled as he caught her eye.

"Hannah, you're all I've thought about since the moment I met you. You make me smile and laugh. I enjoy each moment with you and can't wait to see you again when we're apart. I would be honored if you would be my girlfriend," he declared. Hannah's award winning smile was the best response he could imagine.

"Yes, I'll be your girlfriend!" she proclaimed, jumping into his lap joyously. He leaned in slowly and kissed her lips. Hannah wrapped her arms around his neck and returned his kiss with enthusiasm.

Something stirred within Chace. A deep longing that he hadn't felt before. Not like this. He put his hands on her slender waist and pulled her closer on his lap, one leg on either side of him, and deepened the kiss. Hannah's fingers slowly crept up his neck into his hair. He let out a groan of pleasure as his hands slid around her lower back and down to her thighs. His fingers met the soft skin of her legs and started to travel back up, slipping underneath her dress.

Hannah sat up on her knees, still straddling him, as her hands held his face. She kissed him with passion and desire and Chace felt lightheaded from the intensity of their kiss. His hands slowly made their way up her outer thigh until he could feel the lace material of her panties. Hannah gasped within the kiss as his thumbs made small circles around her lower stomach when his hands gripped her hips.

He moved his hands around and felt the smooth, exposed skin of her backside below her panties. Hannah moaned, disconnecting their heavy kiss. Both of them were panting as they gazed into each others eyes.

"Hannah, if I don't stop now, I don't know if I'll be able to," Chace swallowed, his breath coming in short spurts.

~~*~*~*

Hannah bit her lip, trying to control her breathing as she sat herself back on the couch next to him. Being that close to Chace and feeling him touch her skin was intoxicating. Part of her knew that they were getting a little out of control, but the other part screamed for more. Chace gave her desires that she had never felt before.

"I'm sorry. I should have had better control of myself," she apologized.

"Please don't be sorry. I was just as much to blame, if not more so. I am the man and I don't want you to think of me as someone who would take advantage of you," Chace countered.

"Do you mind if I ask you a question?" she asked, feeling her cheeks grow warm.

"Not at all. What do you want to know?" he replied, leaning back on the couch.

"Have you ever been with someone before?" she inquired. Chace paused for a moment as she waited.

"I've only been with one girl," he answered.

"Was she the girl you moved to Tennessee to be with?" Hannah questioned, already knowing the answer. Chace shook his head yes.

"What about you?" he questioned, putting his arm behind the couch around Hannah's shoulder. She happily rested her head on his strong arm.

"I've only been with one person, one

time," she responded.

Hannah knew she didn't have much experience in that department of life. With her mother dying when she was young, she didn't really get the chance to ask questions. She had been told about the "birds and the bee's" but she had also been a lot younger when her parents had that conversation with her.

Kaylee had done her best to answer her questions, but she didn't know much until after she had married Aaron. They had stayed abstinent for each other until marriage. Hannah wanted to do that, but she caved to a guy she had barely been dating when she as twenty-four.

After a few moments, Hannah glanced over at Chace. He was looking down at her with a look she had never seen him give her. She was about to say something when a knock sounded at his door, causing both of them to jump. Chace got up and looked through the peephole.

"Hey, Jake," he greeted, allowing his friend in.

"What's up, Cha...Oh...Hannah, hi," Jake stuttered. Hannah waved shyly, standing up from the couch.

"I should probably be going now," she announced, grabbing the red velvet box that her necklace had come in.

"No, I didn't mean to interrupt anything. I can come back later," said Jake, fumbling toward the door. Hannah laughed, walking over to Chace.

"I'll see you tomorrow?" she asked, giving him a hug.

"What, you think I'd miss spending Christmas day with my girlfriend?" Chace challenged smiling. Hannah blushed, shooting a quick glance over at Jake. A sly smile played on his face.

"Well, I think I'm going to have breakfast with Kaylee and Aaron, if Kaylee is feeling well enough. Do you want to meet up for lunch?" she asked,

"Yeah, that would be great. Do you mind if the gang comes along? I'm sure they're going to want to hang out," said Chace, looking over to Jake.

"I know Lana would love that. I love my wife, but she sure talks a lot when there isn't another girl to chat back at her," voiced Jake, shaking his head. Chace guided Hannah out into the hallway, leaving Jake in his cabin.

"Merry Christmas Eve," he said sweetly.

"Merry Christmas Eve to you, too. Thank you so much for such a beautiful gift," she said, holding the blue gem in her slim fingers.

"And thank you for all three of your gifts to me," said Chace, waving his eyebrows up and down. Hannah looked at him, puzzled.

"The third was your answer to be mine," he spoke softly.

Hannah smiled, leaning closer to Chace. He pulled her close and kissed her so gently she thought she might melt. He kissed her once more on her forehead as they said their goodnights to each other.

December 27th, 2018

The two days following Christmas Eve were packed full of fun. Christmas day was spent on the ship sailing to their next destination. Hannah had a great time hanging out with Chace and his friends. She really enjoyed talking with Lana and felt like she had known the group for months rather than just a few days.

They had chosen to check out the water attraction on the top deck. There was a slide to go down and they enjoyed a lot of their day soaking up the sun and lounging around the pool.

Later that night Chace had taken her to the top deck to enjoy the Dine-In-Movie-Night. A large screen had been put up and a projector displayed the movie. Chace and Hannah had shared a large bag of popcorn as they sat close to one another watching the movie.

Day six of the cruise had brought them to Ocho Rios, Jamaica. This had been one of Hannah's favorite days because both her group and Chace's group all hung out together, even Hunter. Hannah wasn't as thrilled that Hunter was there, but he kept his distance and seemed to ignore her completely.

The day had been full of adventure. First the combined group had gone snorkeling. Hannah had loved diving and seeing all the marine life right at her fingertips. Dan had brought an underwater camera and had taken some great pictures.

Next on their itinerary was finding a hidden lagoon. The water was almost teal green and a waterfall cascaded down into the lagoon water. The area was shaded by trees and was tucked away like a secret oasis. Everyone had their turn jumping from the waterfall, splashing into the lagoon.

Hannah had loved every moment. She couldn't help smiling every time Chace would touch her, hold her hand, or sneak a kiss from her. She had been elated the night he asked her to be his girlfriend. It felt good adding solidarity to their relationship.

The current day brought the final full day of the cruise. They had been at sea since the previous evening sailing back to New York. Hannah did her best to shove away the feelings of depression at the thought of not seeing Chace. She wanted to enjoy every minute she could of this amazing cruise before it ended.

The air on deck grew cooler with each

passing hour as they made their way north up the east coast of the states. Hannah and Chace were out walking around the deck together late that afternoon.

"Hannah?" he spoke, interrupting her thoughts. She jerked her head in his direction, her face flushing as she realized she wasn't listening to what he had been saying.

"I'm sorry. I was kind of off in my own little world there for a minute," she apologized sheepishly.

"Care to share?" he wanted to know. Hannah grimaced. She didn't want to complain to him about her sadness. But looking at him she knew she could tell him anything.

"I was just thinking about tomorrow," she replied softly. She looked down at her feet as they continued walking. Chace walked quietly in thought.

"What do you think is going to happen tomorrow?" he asked. Hannah looked up at him, puzzled.

"Well, tomorrow we get into New York City and fly to our separate homes, in separate states," she answered glumly. Chace squeezed her hand.

"And what do you think will happen after that?" he probed on.

"Life will continue how it had before the cruise. We'll go back to work, pay bills, eat, sleep, etcetera," said Hannah, the gloominess of her words pulling her downward.

"Yes, we will do all that, but things will be different. You know, when I asked you to be my girlfriend, it wasn't just for the cruise. I take that status change for us seriously in the sense that I want to make every effort to see you when I can. We don't live so far from each other that we can't make this work," he explained, pulling her over to a deck chair. Hannah sat down next to him and gave him a small smile.

"I know you're right. I've just been in such a euphoria here on this cruise with you that it makes me sad to think of all of this coming to an end," she said, looking around the ship.

"Well, the cruise will end, yes, but you and I don't have to. Not if we work together," Chace replied, pulling her into a hug. Hannah knew he was right and that she shouldn't be letting herself get down about the cruise ending.

At least not for now, she thought to herself.

Ominous dark clouds rolled over the cruise ship as Hannah and Chace made their way inside. Cold droplets of rain touched her face before she stepped through the door. Even the weather reflected her mood.

That night was the last formal night and Hannah needed to get ready. Before getting off on her floor, Chace pulled her close and kissed her passionately. She became lightheaded and felt dizzy as the elevator stopped.

"Don't forget what we talked about on the deck, okay?" he whispered, looking into her eyes. Hannah saw honesty and truth and she knew she could trust him about wanting the relationship to continue, even when the cruise had finished.

Hannah wanted to do something pretty

with her hair again, so she asked if Kaylee would do up her hair in a fashionable style. As always, Kaylee delivered a stunning hair do. Hannah smiled brightly at the half up, half down do. Her hair lay in ringlets down her shoulders and back, and Kaylee side-swept her bangs perfectly.

"What jewelry are you going to wear?" Kaylee asked, spraying a final touch of hairspray.

"I want to wear the necklace Chace got me for Christmas, but I don't have any earrings that match with it," she replied.

"Here, why don't you wear my diamond earrings? Your pendant has a diamond on it so that will look really nice together," Kaylee smiled, handing Hannah a pair of sparkling diamond earrings.

"Kaylee, I can't wear these! Didn't Aaron give them to you as a ten year anniversary gift?" asked Hannah, staring at the gorgeous earring set. Kaylee smiled cheerfully.

"Yes, he did. But you're my sister and I know you'll take care of them for tonight," she answered. Hannah carefully slipped the earrings in her lobes and clasped the necklace Chace had given her around her neck.

"Go get your dress on. I want to see how everything fits together," Kaylee instructed, excitedly.

Hannah went to her closet and pulled out the black dress she had saved for the formal evening. Slipping on the classy, snug dress, she was careful not to disturb her hair. Zipping up the dress from the side, she pulled out her black lace stilettos slipping them on.

"You take forever!" Kaylee pretended to whine.

"That's because you're impatient," laughed Hannah, turning the corner so her sister could see. Kaylee's eyes went wide as she looked her sister over from head to toe.

"You look just like Mom," Kaylee beamed. Hannah looked in the mirror and for the first time that day her spirits felt lifted. Excitement for the evening grew as butterflies flew wildly in her stomach.

~~*~*~*

Chace heard a knock at his door. He adjusted his bow tie in the mirror before going to open the door.

"Hey Chace," greeted Lana smiling. She was wearing a long maroon dress. Jake and Dan were in the hallway behind her dressed in their suits.

"Lana, you're looking stunning as always," Chace complimented her, kissing her hand. Lana laughed lightly.

"Jake, you could learn some pointers from Chace," she joked, looking back at her husband.

"Go woo your own girl," Jake bantered, taking Lana's hand.

Chace's group headed to the elevator. He was looking forward to this formal night dinner more than the last. This time Hannah's group was going to sit with his group. Chace broke off from his friends to meet Hannah at her cabin.

Just as he was about to knock on her door, the handle turned and Kaylee almost bumped into him.

"Oh! Hey, Chace," she said, sashaying around him in her light purple dress. Her hair, the exact color as Hannah's, had been pinned up in an elaborate style.

"It's amazing what women can do with their hair," he commented, looking at her intricate braids and curls meshing together in harmony. Kaylee laughed.

"I *love* it! That's why I became a hair stylist," she stated.

Aaron came out of his cabin and walked the few steps to where Kaylee and Chace were talking. He put his arm around Kaylee lovingly and swooped down to kiss her cheek.

"Is everybody ready?" he asked, looking between them.

"Ready," confirmed a voice behind Chace. He turned to see Hannah standing in the doorway smoothing out her dress.

Chace's heart kicked into high gear. He was staring at the most beautiful creature God could have ever created. The way her hair was partly piled onto her head, the rest falling down in curly ringlets, made her face look soft and warm. The black sleeveless dress she wore looked as though it was sewn onto her. Lastly, he noticed that she wore his necklace he gave her for Christmas. Chace was speechless.

"Hey, Chace," she greeted quietly, her cheeks flushing a bright pink.

"Hannah...you...*wow*!" was all he managed to utter. Kaylee snickered in the background as Hannah's cheeks grew darker. Chace shook his head to regain composure. He held out his hand for Hannah to take. She smiled happily and accepted his hand.

"Where is your group?" asked Kaylee.

"They are already at the table. I just came by here to escort this beautiful woman to dinner," he answered, pulling Hannah closer to him.

Before the group departed for the elevator, the door behind Chace burst open. Out stumbled Hunter dressed in a dark blue suit with a light blue tie that was crooked. His hair was coiffed in a way that suggested he either didn't care, or had tried too hard. He also supported a five o'clock shadow.

"Hunter, are you alright?" asked Aaron, walking over to his friend. Hunter straightened himself as best he could.

"Right as rain, my friend," he replied grinning widely. Kaylee walked up to him and fixed his tie.

"Trying something new with your hair?" she asked, stepping back. Hunter laughed loudly.

"Yeah, I just kind of threw it together last minute," he explained, patting the sides of his hair swaying a bit.

"Hunter, are you drunk?" asked Aaron flatly.

"I might have had a few," he answered slyly, his gaze wandering over to Hannah. The way his eyes roved over her body made the hair on the back of Chace's neck raise.

"Hannah Lane. My, my how you've grown

up. You're are magnificent!" Hunter complimented, reaching out as if to touch her hair. Chace tensed, moving himself in front of her.

"Oookay, Hunter. Let's get down to dinner, shall we?" suggested Kaylee, pulling Hunter by his outstretched arm. Hunter looked as though he wanted to protest, but Aaron came up beside him and helped move him along.

Chace breathed out a small sigh and he could feel Hannah relax beside him as well. He hadn't thought about Hunter coming to the dinner with them.

He thought back to when they were in Jamaica. The two groups of friends had spent the day together, including Hunter. It was uncomfortable at first, but Hunter generally seemed to ignore Hannah, so Chace didn't mind so much.

"Should we go?" asked Hannah, breaking him out of his thoughts. He smiled down at her lovely face and guided her to dinner, her arm in his.

~~*~*~*

All throughout dinner, Hunter watched as Hannah and Chace sat together, laughing and smiling at each other. Even in his drunken stupor, he knew that he would never get her to give him a chance now. Aaron had told him that Hannah and Chace were a couple, and that meant she was off limits.

Hunter had spent most of the day drinking in his room. First, he had frequented a couple bars before deciding it would be better to be alone. But before long he realized being alone with his thoughts wasn't exactly what he needed either, so he started to drink in his room to try and get Hannah off of his mind.

Now here he was, sitting a few seats away from her and he couldn't push her out of his head. Reaching for his flute of champagne, he downed it quickly. Her beauty filled his sight. From her perfectly styled hair down to her sexy black heels, she was all he ever wanted in a woman.

Yes, all I ever wanted, but all of which can't have, he thought bitterly.

A waiter came around and Hunter asked him for a glass of red wine. As the waiter set off on his task, Hunter found himself eye to eye with Aaron. The look on his friend's face was that of worry and confusion. Hunter ignored it.

"I really think you've had too much," whispered Aaron, leaning in toward him. Hunter scoffed at Aaron's allegation.

"Aaron, it's the last night of the cruise. Why not go out with a bang?" he sneered. He knew that was a lame excuse for why he was drinking, but he wasn't going to tell Aaron the real reason.

The waiter came back with Hunter's glass of red wine and he drank generously from it.

"Leave the bottle," he instructed to the waiter. The balding man sat the bottle down on the table in front of him and excused himself. Aaron looked at him with concern etched on his face. Hunter took another drink.

"Buddy, I think you need to stop," Aaron advised quietly, setting the bottle of wine farther away from Hunter. He knew that Aaron was only trying to look after him, but he didn't care at this point.

He heard Hannah's laughter floating through the air and he glanced over to her. She was leaning on Chace laughing at something Kaylee had said. Chace had his arm around her as he laughed along with her. She looked up at Chace and he bent down to kiss her softly. The bliss on Hannah's face as they broke the short kiss was all it took to make Hunter snap.

"I need to leave," he announced to Aaron, after chugging one last large gulp of wine, emptying his glass. Hunter stood up too quickly and felt the room spin. He teetered and gripped his chair to steady himself. Aaron stood up abruptly to make sure his friend didn't fall. This caused everyone at the table to cast their eyes on Hunter and Aaron. Hunter locked his gaze with Hannah and he saw what he thought was pity in her eyes. Pity for him.

"Come on, Hunter. I'll take you back to your cabin," offered Aaron, tugging on his arm. Hunter jerked his arm away forcefully.

"No," he growled. He turned and left the table on his own. He stumbled once on a woman's chair, but regained his composure before exiting the dining room.

Once he was out of the room, Hunter ran his fingers through his hair. He had made a scene at the table, but he didn't care. Everything seemed to be spiraling out of control for him. He didn't understand why he felt he needed Hannah so much, but he couldn't get her to leave his mind. Not knowing what else to do, Hunter went in search of the nearest lounge.

~~*~*~*

Dinner flew by for Hannah. Sitting with all of her new friends and with her family, everything felt perfect. One thing that stuck out in her mind was when Hunter made a hasty retreat. She knew he had been drinking before dinner and she saw him consume even more alcohol at the table. Hannah was concerned when he refused to let Aaron help him.

"Well, as much as I wanted dessert before, I think I'm going to have to call it quits for tonight," Kaylee announced, getting up from her seat. Aaron took the last bite of his meal and stood up with her. A round of goodnights ensued as the couple left the table.

Hannah stayed with Chace and his friends as the fun continued. She didn't want it to end. But after another hour of talking, laughing at picking at desserts, the group finally announced that they were heading back to their cabins.

"We'll see you in the morning, right?" asked Lana, looking over to Hannah.

"Yes, of course," she said, giving her a hug. Dan, Jake and Lana said their goodbyes for the night, leaving Hannah and Chace to themselves at the table.

"Do you want to walk around the ship with me, my lady?" he asked, helping Hannah out of her chair.

"Yeah, I would love that. But first I need to change. I don't want to make the mistake of walking around in my heels again," she giggled.

"As much as I am loving your dress and shoes tonight, I know that it wouldn't be very comfortable for you. I should change, too," said Chace, looking down at his black suit.

The couple walked out of the room to the hallway. Hannah heard a faint pelting noise coming from the window. She walked over to the window and saw rain coming down in sheets lit by the deck light.

"Well, I don't think we'll be walking outside tonight," she observed, pointing to the window. Chace followed her gaze and saw the rain.

"Yeah. It probably would have been too cold out anyway. We can still walk around inside, though," he suggested.

"Sounds good to me. Want to meet up in the atrium?" she asked.

"Sure thing, beautiful. See you soon," he stated, kissing her forehead.

Hannah approached her cabin and reached into her small black sequence purse to retrieve her key. As she swiped the key into the door, a strong arm wrapped around her stomach while a hand slid across her mouth. Panic ran her blood cold as she dropped the key card on the hallway floor.

"Don't fight me, okay?" whispered a familiar voice behind her, his breath reeking of alcohol. Shock rendered her still as she realized who had grabbed her.

"Hunter?" she tried to say through his

hand, but it only came out muffled. Hunter forced her to walk backward and she heard him fiddle with his door. Fear gripped her chest. He was pulling her into his cabin.

Once inside, Hunter released her suddenly, causing Hannah to fall forward onto a couch. Gathering her bearings, she looked around his cabin. There was only one small light coming from the bathroom around the corner. From that light, she could see numerous beer bottles scattered haphazardly around the floor.

"Sorry I'm not very tidy," Hunter spoke harshly.

Hannah looked over at him with irritation burning in her eyes. His suit jacket was off and his tie was askew. His hair was going in every which direction.

"What are you doing?" she asked, standing up from the couch, crossing her arms over her chest. She was getting tired of these run-ins with Hunter. But the smile that crept onto his face made her confident stance falter.

What IS he doing, she thought as Hunter walked toward her slowly. He had picked up a beer from somewhere and took a drink as he came closer. The look in his eyes took away any ounce of defense she had left. Her knees started to tremble as he came within inches of her face.

"What I'm *doing* is taking what I want. Being the nice guy obviously didn't work, so maybe you'll like bad-boy Hunter instead," he commented, the stench of his breath causing Hannah's stomach to turn. She tried to maneuver past him, but his arm went out in a flash and caught her in the ribs.

"No, no, no. You can't get away that easily," he said in a singsong voice.

With one swift movement, Hunter threw Hannah onto his bed several feet away. She landed on her back, her head jerking with the force of the rough motion. Hunter knelt onto the bed unbuttoning the first two buttons of his shirt. Alarm bells clanged furiously in her head.

No! This can't be happening! Hannah's mind screamed.

She scrambled to the top of his bed trying to get away from him. Hunter reached out and pulled her legs, forcing her closer to him. His hands crept up her thighs as he grabbed her dress, pushing it higher on her legs. Hannah tried to stop him, but he pinned her hands down with his own.

"Don't make me do something you'll regret," he declared darkly.

With one hand still clasped to her wrist, Hunter's other hand explored the fabric of her dress up her stomach to her chest. He situated himself so that he was straddling her, both his hands now free.

His greedy hands roamed her chest, stopping on her breasts. Hannah tried to wiggle herself free, but couldn't move under Hunters weight. A crazed smile lit his face and Hannah shivered. He gripped the fabric of her dress in the middle of her chest.She gasped as he ripped her dress part way down her chest. Tears fell generously from her eyes.

"Hunter, *please* don't do this!" she begged, her body shaking in fear. She knew what would happen if he didn't stop. Adrenaline pumped through her veins as she tried to think of a way to stop him.

He bent over on top of her and lowered his head to her ear. His hot breath tickled her neck as she tried to move her head away.

"This wouldn't have been so bad if you had just given me a chance," he stated before starting a trail of kisses down her neck.

Hunter's tongue licked her collarbone and his kisses began to move upward again. Hannah's hands slowly roamed around the bed, trying not to draw attention to him. She was looking for something, anything to grab that she could hit him with. Suddenly her fingers touched something cold and cylindrical. Hannah realized she had found an empty beer bottle.

Perfect! she thought, getting a good grip on the glass bottle.

Hannah held the neck of the bottle and mentally prepared herself for the task she was about to do. She had never hit anyone before, let alone strike someone with a beer bottle. Hunter's lips found hers and he kissed her fervently. She squeezed her eyes shut as she drew the bottle up intending to hit his head. She moved her arm out to swing, but as she did Hunter shifted his position higher up on her body. With the beer bottle already in motion, Hannah knew she was going to miss his head. A thud-like noise resounded from the bottle as it hit his back.

Hunter drew himself up from kissing her and looked at her baffled. It was darker in the corner where they were and she saw him look for what hit him. His hand touched hers, still attached to the glass bottle. As he felt its shape, she heard him growl.

"I told you not to do anything stupid!" he bellowed. Hannah cringed as he drew his hand up and violently backhanded her in the mouth. She cried out in pain as blood entered her mouth from her lip. She could feel that he had split her lip open.

"Now look what you made me do!" he yelled, holding her jaw tightly in his hand.

Hannah was about to shove him when she remembered the beer bottle was still in her hand. Hunter hadn't taken it from her. With a last ditch effort, she gathered all the strength she could and hurled the bottle toward his head. This time it connected with its intended target, crashing open on the side of his head.

Hunter fell to the side and off the bed, freeing Hannah. She didn't know if he was unconscious so she jumped up as fast as she could and fled for the door. When she opened the door, she heard a low guttural sound behind her. She turned back and saw Hunter slowly getting off the floor holding his head. When he saw her he immediately darted after her, tripping over another beer bottle on the floor.

Hannah wanted to bang on her sister's door, but retracted that thought almost instantly. The last thing she wanted was to get her sister involved in a fight. She didn't know if Hunter would attack Kaylee, so she did the next best thing. She ran.

~~*~*~*

Chace sat in the atrium dressed in jeans and a gray sweatshirt. He had been there for almost a twenty minutes waiting for Hannah. He knew it would take her a little longer to change since she had a dress on and her hair done up, but twenty minutes was stretching it.

Maybe I should go see if everything is okay, he thought, gazing up to the spacious atrium ceiling.

Chace could see deck four clearly from where he was sitting. Deck five was a more out of his sight. But as he looked at deck five he saw something peculiar flash by every foot or so. He saw red curly hair wave over the banister as if someone was running. He could hear a click clack sound echoing throughout the atrium.

Suddenly a figure grasped the railing and looked around the atrium frantically. His heart skipped a beat when he realized it was Hannah. Confusion swept through him as he saw that she was still wearing her dress. He couldn't see her clearly, but he saw the color and recognized the off the shoulder design.

What is she doing? he wondered. He saw Hannah looking around as if trying to find someone.

"Hannah," he called out to her, cupping his mouth with his hands. She looked down to where he was and he smiled up to her. But her face was anything but happy. Her lips were red and she looked scared. Did she have lipstick on?

Hannah's attention was drawn away from him as she turned to look behind her. She turned quickly back to Chace, panic distorting her features.

All of the sudden, she disappeared. He could hear the click clack sound again, but he couldn't see her. Chace stood up about ready to go after her when he saw a man run by the railing where Hannah was just at. The man was tall enough for him to be able to make out his face. It was Hunter. Hunter was chasing Hannah.

White hot anger coursed through him as Chace bolted for the stairs. He ran as fast as he could, almost colliding with an elderly couple. When he made it to deck five, he ran in the same direction as he saw Hunter just moments ago.

Chace had no idea where they had gone. He made quick glances inside the bars, casinos, and shops to see if he could catch sight of them, but his efforts were fruitless. He stopped at the double doors that led outside. He didn't think Hannah would go out there, but before he turned away, he noticed a red drop on the door handle. Dread seized him. Who was bleeding?

Chace slammed through the doors and was greeted with a fierce wind blowing cold rain in his face. The deck was dark, only lit every few yards by deck lights illuminating the back of the deck chairs. Not knowing which way they went, Chace started running toward the back of the ship. The rain felt like it was slicing through his skin.

"Hannah!" he shouted through the dark rain. The wind howled and he doubted his voice could be heard more then a foot away. The ship swayed slightly with the wind.

Come on, Hannah. Where are you? he thought trying to balance himself on a deck chair.

Chace approached the stern where two large lights lit up the deck. He searched frantically through the chairs to see if she was hiding among them. As he lifted one of the upturned deck chairs he saw her crouched in the fetal position. She squinted into the light.

"Leave me alone!" she screamed, hiding her face in her arms.

Chase knelt down and put his hands on her bare shoulders. Her skin was ice cold as she struggled against him.

"Hannah, it's Chace!" he shouted over the wind.

Hannah stopped her efforts of escape and looked up again. He saw recognition in her eyes. She burst into his arms, knocking him over on the deck. He wrapped his arms around her tightly before pulling her back.

Hannah's hair was flattened to her head by the rain and her black dress was soaked. He noticed that the front of her dress had been ripped. The red he had noticed on her lips earlier was not lipstick. It was blood. Her lower lip was swollen and cut. Blood had dripped down her chin mixing with the rain.

Chace pulled her up gently and guided her underneath a lit canvas awning by a window. Hannah shivered violently in his arms.

"We need to get you inside," he said loudly against the wind. A large gust of wind caused the ship to sway. They were both tossed in different directions. Chace slammed into the wall and Hannah flew forward into a deck chair. Righting himself, Chace quickly went to assist Hannah back toward the wall.

Before they could make it to a door, Chace felt Hannah being wrenched out of his arms. He heard her scream out in pain as she collided with a small table. He turned around and saw Hunter coming straight for him. Hunter's fist swung at him and landed on his cheek, causing Chace to fall back. Pain ripped through his face as he tried to shake himself off.

Hunter stalked toward Hannah and grabbed her by the arm roughly. She winced and tried to pull away from him, but he was too strong. Rage burned through Chace.

"Hunter, get your hands off her!" He yelled, bolting toward him. He rammed into Hunter full force, knocking him over. Hunter got up and glared at Chace.

"You know what, Chace? You can have her! That ginger *slut* isn't worth it anymore!" Hunter scoffed.

Chace saw red. He ran toward Hunter and pounced on top of him throwing his fist into Hunter's face. Hunter roared out in agony and started to grab Chace by the collar of his sweatshirt, but someone lifted Chace off of Hunter. He looked over and saw a few members of the crew separating them.

"What's going on here!" shouted a burly bald man, looking over at Hannah.

"This man attacked me!" she yelled, rain soaking her slight frame.

"Okay, let's take this inside," said

another crew member, pulling Hunter to his feet.

Once inside, blankets were fetched for the three waterlogged individuals. Hunter had been detained as someone tended to his broken nose. As Chace sat listening to Hannah retell what happened, his fists balled up, furry festering in his gut. Hunter had tried to rape her. He pulled her close to him as she trembled.

The bald security guard looked over at Hunter, his eyes hard as flint. He nodded to the other security guard to take Hunter away.

"How did you know we were out there?" Chace heard Hannah ask quietly.

"We have security cameras placed throughout the ship and we saw you running away from that man," the guard answered, pointing to Hunter's retreating frame.

"When we saw you all head out on deck we felt there was a situation unfolding that needed tending to," he finished, writing something down on his pad of paper.

"What will happen to him now?" Chace inquired.

"Well, we'll keep him in confined quarters until we dock tomorrow in New York. The NYPD will take it up from there," the security guard informed them. Chace nodded his head and looked down at Hannah. Her lip had stopped bleeding.

"Are we free to go?" Chace asked, wanting to get Hannah into dry clothes before she froze to death.

"Yes, I have all the information I need from you. The police will be in contact with you if you feel the need to press charges," he explained.

"Thank you," Hannah responded. The security guard nodded.

Chace and Hannah walked silently to the elevator. The only sound came from her heels clicking on the floor. He held her tight as the elevator opened to her floor.

"Oh no," Hannah groaned as they got closer to her cabin. Chace looked down at her with concern.

"What's wrong?" he asked softly.

"I don't have my key card for my room. In my struggle with Hunter, I dropped it," she replied, her shoulders slumping.

When they got to her cabin, both of them looked around on the hallway floor to see if it had dropped somewhere nearby. Neither of them could find it. Chace saw Hannah gaze over at her sister's cabin door. She drew in a deep breath and let it out in a huff.

"I guess I should tell my sister."

~~*~*~*

Hannah knocked on the door to Kaylee and Aaron's cabin. Aaron answered, alarm on his face as he saw Hannah and Chace in their state of disarray.

"Oh my gosh! What *happened*!?" Aaron questioned, exchanging looks between the two of them.

"Long story. Mind if we come in?" asked Chace, his arm around Hannah's waist. Aaron moved aside and let them in. Hannah was grateful to see that she had not woken them. Kaylee looked up from her book, her eyes bulging when she saw them.

"Hannah! Oh my gosh, Hannah! What the heck happened to you?" Kaylee cried, holding Hannah's face in her hands. Hannah shivered.

"Before we get into it, do you have some clothes I could borrow?" she asked, looking down at her ruined dress.

"Well, actually, I found your key card outside your door. I figured you had dropped it on accident and you'd come to me," Kaylee remarked, grabbing Hannah's key off of the dresser.

"Oh, thank God! Do you mind if I change real fast?" she asked.

"No, but be quick. I need to know what happened," Kaylee declared.

Hannah and Chace went over to her room and unlocked the door. She sighed in relief that her sister had found her key. Walking over to her dresser, she pulled out pink and gray flannel pants and a long sleeved pink shirt.

"I'll just be a minute," she called over her shoulder.

Chace sat on the edge of her bed. Hannah started to unzip her dress, but realized that the zipper wouldn't budge much more than a fourth of the way down. She yanked and pulled trying to get the zipper to release. Hannah bit her lip and let out a small cry. She had forgotten about the cut on her lip. Thankfully, it didn't start bleeding.

"Hannah? Are you okay?" asked Chace

"Yes, I'm okay, but I can't get my dress unzipped. The zipper is stuck," she replied, coming around the corner. She pointed under her arm where the zipper was. Chace came over and pulled downward on the zipper, not getting anywhere.

"We might need to cut it," he suggested.

"That's okay. It's ruined anyway," she responded, pointing to the rip at the front of her dress.

Hannah went over to her bathroom and grabbed a small pair of scissors from the drawer, handing them to Chace. He made a small cut parallel to the zipper and was able to free the zipper from the fabric, pulling it the rest of the way down. Hannah looked at him and saw that his face had turned red as he snuck a peak at her newly exposed skin near her breast. She couldn't help but smile a little at his expression.

"Thank you," she said shyly, retreating to the bathroom to change her clothes.

Once Hannah was dressed and had untangled her hair, they went back over to Kaylee's room. Kaylee and Aaron sat on their bed while Chace and Hannah sat on the couch across from them.

"Okay, so start from the top. What happened?" Kaylee grilled. Hannah sighed, not wanting to tell her sister about the attack. She knew it would upset her.

"Hunter attacked me outside of my cabin on my way back from dinner. He forced me into his room and tried to...rape me," Hannah stated. She would have continued, but Aaron shot off the bed.

"He did *WHAT*?!" yelled Aaron, a vein popping out on his forehead. Hannah glanced at Kaylee seeing her hands fly over her mouth in horror.

"How could he do that?" asked Kaylee, removing her hands.

"Where is he now?" inquired Aaron, venom lacing his words.

Hannah told them the rest of the story, eventually answering Aaron's question. When she was finished both Kaylee and Aaron were speechless. It was a lot harder for her to tell them than it was the security guard. It was more personal and Hannah found herself crying softly as Chace held her in his arms.

"Are you going to press charges?" asked Kaylee, handing Hannah a tissue. She accepted the tissue and blew her nose.

"I don't know. He was obviously inebriated beyond belief. Would he have done something like that if he had been his normal self?" Hannah asked Aaron.

"I've known him for a long time. Yes, he is strong willed and generally gets what he's after, but I would have never believed he would be capable of something like this," Aaron responded, sitting down next to Kaylee.

"I guess just think about it. You've dealt with enough tonight. Do you want to stay in here with us?" Kaylee asked, looking up at Aaron for confirmation.

"Thanks, but I'm only right next door. If I need you I know I can come over," answered Hannah, holding Chace's hand. He squeezed it lovingly, making Hannah feel warm.

"Chace, thank you so much for being there for Hannah. I don't know what would have happened if you hadn't been there," said Kaylee, expressing her gratitude. She got up and hugged him fiercely.

"Hannah is like a little sister to me, and knowing that she has someone who will protect her means a lot. You're a good guy, Chace," thanked Aaron, adding his two cents in.

Hannah smiled happily. It made her feel good to know that Kaylee and Aaron both approved of Chace.

"Not a problem. She's worth the fight," Chace winked at Hannah, making her blush.

"Well, off with you two. You both need to get some rest," stated Kaylee, shooing them to the door. Hannah hugged her sister and brother-in-law. She felt so blessed to have such a loving support system in her life.

"Are you going to be okay?" asked Chace once they were in front of Hannah's cabin. She wanted to be strong, and she knew she was safe with her sister and Aaron next door to her.

"I'll be alright. Thank you so much for being my knight in shining armor tonight," she replied, putting her arms around his shoulders. He smiled down at her, causing her insides to flip and flop.

"Anytime, my fair maiden. I'll always be here for you," he said, his voice a whisper by the end of his statement. Hannah closed her eyes as he lowered his forehead to rest on hers.

"Sleep well," he breathed softly.

Hannah tilted her head up and met his

lips with hers. Chace tightened his grip around her and kissed her passionately. Suddenly, he stopped and pulled back.

"I didn't hurt your lip, did I?" he asked, tracing his thumb along her cut. Hannah giggled.

"No, you didn't. And even if you had, kissing you is worth a little pain," she stated, smiling up at him. He chuckled and kissed her once more.

"Good night, good night! Parting is such sweet sorrow, that I shall say good night till it be morrow," said Chace, quoting the famous Shakespearian line from Romeo and Juliet.

"Till the morrow," Hannah whispered back.

~~*~*~*

Chace tossed and turned that night. Visions of Hannah bleeding from her lip and shivering in the cold rain invaded his thoughts, robbing him of the sleep he so desperately needed.

Unable to get comfortable, he got up and went to the sink to splash some water on his face. He had been so tempted to ask Hannah if she wanted him to stay with her. She looked like she was trying to be brave, and he knew there was nothing to worry about now that Hunter was being held by security.

Chace wandered back to his bed and sat down with a huff. He picked up his phone to see what time it was. Hannah's picture brightened up his background and he got lost looking at her eyes. He knew deep down in his heart that he loved her.

A light knock sounded at his door. Knowing it was late, Chace could only hope it was one person. And there she was as he opened the door. Hannah stood before him in short pink and gray pajama shorts and the same pink shirt he had seen her in when he left. Her hair was down in perfect red ringlets. A smile crept onto his face.

"I can't sleep, and I thought..." Hannah began, before he put his finger up to her lips.

Without saying a word Chace pulled her gently into his room, shutting the door quietly. He engulfed her small frame in a hug that she reciprocated in full. He could feel her shoulders shaking as she cried softly into his shirt.

In one swift movement, Chace picked her up, their embrace never breaking. Hannah's legs wrapped loosely around his waist as he took her over to his bed. He turned out the light and effortlessly set her down on his bed. She released her grip on him and he moved onto the bed next to her. As he pulled the blankets over them, she shifted her body closer to his, both lying down as they faced each other.

Hannah reached out and cupped his cheek. She pulled herself against him and kissed him softly. Chace wrapped his arm around her, his hand caressing her backside and sliding down to her bare legs. Her skin was soft and smooth. Her arm wrapped around his neck deepening the kiss.

Chace's hand slid to her backside again, this time giving a little squeeze. Her body reacted by swaying her hips against him. A dangerous move. Excitement flared within him. He moved his kisses down her jawline to her shoulder and then back to the base of her neck, breathing her name in the hollow of her throat. A small moan escaped from Hannah's lips.

Chace grabbed her hip and lightly pushed her onto her back as he pivoted his body partially over hers. Hannah's arms went above her head resting on the pillow, her hair splayed everywhere. Through the small window by his bed, moonlight softly illuminated her face. The storm had ended.

Gazing into her eyes, Chace knew if he wanted he could have her. He knew in *his* heart that it would be for love, but glancing down at her split lip caused him to pause. Hannah had experienced a horrifying ordeal only hours ago. He didn't want such a big decision to be made after what she had just gone through. And there was also the question of if she loved him or not.

Chace bent down and kissed her lips tenderly before rolling himself back onto his side next to her. She positioned herself facing him, her head resting on her hand.

"Thanks for letting me stay with you tonight. I didn't want to be alone after...you know," said Hannah, tracing imaginary lines on the bed.

"No worries. I'm glad you came," he smiled as he watched her yawn.

Chace pulled her to him so her back was against his chest. He put his arm around her securely and kissed the back of her neck. Hannah put her arm on top of his arm, and within minutes he could feel the deep rhythm of her breathing. Chace closed his eyes and soon fell asleep peacefully next to her.

December 28th, 2018

Hannah woke up and looked around at the room. Something was off. Wasn't her bed along the other wall? She started to turn but was halted by a strong arm resting on her waist. Quickly she looked behind her and saw Chace's tranquil face sleeping. She had forgotten that she stayed with him the previous night.

She turned slowly, not wanting to wake him up just yet. She was able to keep his arm resting on her as she turned to face him. His face was so handsome as he slept. She couldn't help but smile being so close to him.

An alarm went off on Chace's phone and Hannah watched his eyes flutter open. After a few blinks he smiled over at her. The way he looked at her created a storm of butterflies in her stomach.

"A guy could get used to this view each morning," he said, his voice raspy from sleep. Hannah giggled as she sat up. Chace turned over to silence his phone.

"It's about eight o'clock," he announced, running his fingers through his disheveled hair. Hannah tried to hold in her disappointment as it dawned on her that today was the day the cruise ended.

"I should probably get back to my cabin," she stated, sliding to the end of the bed. She slipped on her sandals and checked to make sure her key card was still in her pocket.

"What time do you guys debark?" Chace asked, coming up behind her.

"I think we'll be called around ten o'clock," she replied. She watched as Chace pursed his lips in thought.

"We aren't going to be called until eleven," he said quietly to himself.

Sadness rose within Hannah's heart. They wouldn't even be allowed to leave the ship together. Was now the time she would have to say goodbye? She wasn't ready yet.

"What time does your flight leave?" he asked.

"Um, I think we board around one-thirty," she answered. Chace smiled at her.

"That's perfect! My flight doesn't leave until three o'clock. Why don't we meet up at the airport, and I'll wait with you in the terminal before you go through security. I'll have plenty of time to get to my gate and meet up with my friends on the plane," he explained animatedly. Hannah smiled at his idea.

"That's actually a great idea! Since I'll be at the airport first you can call me when you get there if we can't find each other," she suggested, feeling the dark cloud over her head dissipate a bit.

"Sounds like a plan, beautiful. I guess I'll see you in a few hours," Chace responded, walking with her to the door.

Hannah stopped and turned toward him as she entered the hallway. Chace leaned against the door frame, smiling at her. Even though this new plan delayed their goodbyes, Hannah still couldn't fully get rid of the sad feeling in the pit of her stomach.

"I'll call you when I get to the airport, okay?" Chace reassured her. Hannah nodded, pasting a superficial smile on her face. He took the few steps needed to close the distance between them and put his hands up to her jaw.

"Can I kiss the girl?" he quoted, using the question he had for the first night he kissed her. Hannah felt a small tear form in her eye.

"Yes," she whispered.

Chace leaned in and kissed her ardently. Hannah wrapped her arms around his neck and pulled her body close to his. She could feel him chuckle within the kiss as he picked her up off the floor.

"See you soon, Chace," she spoke softly as their kiss broke. He set her back down on the floor and kissed her forehead.

"Bye, Hannah," he responded.

Hannah headed for the elevator. She turned back once and saw him wave at her. Waving back, she sighed. Only five hours until she could see him again.

Five long hours, she lamented.

Hannah made short work of packing. Once she made sure she had everything, she made her way to Kaylee's cabin.

"Hey, Hannah. How are you feeling today?" asked Aaron, greeting her with a hug.

"I'm doing alright. I'm all packed and thought that I'd wait in your cabin until they call us," said Hannah, setting her luggage down by the door.

"Where is Kaylee?" she asked, looking around the room.

"She's in the bathroom. The baby is giving her morning sickness," Aaron answered, glancing toward the bathroom door.

Hannah noticed how tenderly Aaron spoke of the baby. She knew that he was going to be a great father. Thinking of Kaylee being a mother made Hannah think of her mother. She knew their mother would have been so excited to be a grandmother.

"Oh, Hannah, I didn't know you were in here," Kaylee commented as she exited the bathroom. Her hair was in a messy bun and she still had her pajamas on.

"You okay?" Hannah asked, bringing her sister a bottled water. Drinking generously, Kaylee nodded her head.

"I'm good. I'll be happy when morning sickness isn't on the agenda anymore," she mentioned, walking over to help Aaron pack the rest of their belongings.

Before long Hannah's group was called to proceed to deck three with their luggage.

Hannah exited the cabin first, followed by Aaron. Kaylee came out last with two small carry-on bags. Hannah's heart felt heavy as they made their way to deck three. This cruise had been so much more than she had ever dreamed it would be. But now it was ending.

"May I see your key card please?" asked the crew member by the exit door. Hannah pulled her card out of her pants pocket.

"Alright, thank you so much for traveling with us! We hope you enjoyed your stay," he smiled, handing Hannah her key card back. She looked up at him confused for a moment.

"Aren't you suppose to take these?" she asked, holding out key card.

"Nope. I can take it if you would like, but people usually like to keep them," he informed her.

As Hannah stepped out onto the gangway, she was greeted with a cold wind and little flakes of snow danced around her head. It was a polar opposite of what she had just seen for the past week. Yet another reality check that her perfect vacation was over.

They made it through the cruise terminal fairly smoothly and out into the wintry weather to hail a cab. Hannah shivered as they loaded their luggage into the taxi van. The drive to the airport was quiet. Hannah was lost in her own thoughts, all of which were centered around Chace. Looking out at the snowy landscape, it almost seemed as if the Caribbean cruise was just a dream.

Once at the airport, everyone made their way to their security checkpoint after dropping off their luggage at the terminal desk. Checking her phone Hannah saw that it was eleven thirty.

"Hey, guys, I'm going to hang back. Chace said that he would meet me here once he got to the airport," Hannah informed, setting her carry-on bag down on a chair.

"It won't be too close to boarding time, will it?" asked Kaylee.

"No, he should be here soon I would think," she replied.

"Okay, well, just come find us when you're done," Kaylee smiled.

Hannah sat and watched people milling around the airport. Businessmen, families with small children, and stewardess's/pilots all flocked here and there. She unzipped her heavy jacket allowing it to slack down her arms. Looking down, she noticed her necklace that Chace had given her. She turned it in all directions to watch the light catch the surface.

"That looks like a pretty special necklace," commented a voice beside her. Hannah looked up and saw Chace smiling down at her. She jumped up and threw herself into his embrace. Chuckling emitted from his friends standing behind them.

"What terminal are you heading to?" asked Lana, hugging Hannah after Chace let go.

"I'm going to terminal A," Hannah replied, checking her flight ticket.

"Hey, that's our terminal, too!" Lana announced happily. Hannah looked over to Chace as he nodded.

"Well, that works out perfect. At least we

don't have to hang out here by security for the rest of the time," Hannah stated.

Everyone got into the security checkpoint line and waited as they inched forward every few moments. Chace held Hannah's hand and kept her tightly by his side. For now she felt like she would be okay. Having him with her always made everything seem brighter.

"Okay, so what is your gate number?" Chace asked Hannah as they put their shoes back on.

"I am at gate A7," Hannah answered, picking up her carry-on bag.

"I'm not too far from that. My gate is A5. Why don't we go sit by your gate since you're flight leaves first," he suggested.

"That works for me," she smiled.

"We are going to go sit at our gate. It was really nice to meet you, Hannah. I hope we can hang out again soon," said Lana, squeezing Hannah tightly.

"It was really good to meet you, too. I hope you guys have a safe flight back to Tennessee," replied Hannah, waving to Jake and Dan. Each nodded their goodbyes to her and went on their way.

~~*~*~*

Chace walked Hannah to her gate so she could place her carry-on bag with Kaylee and Aaron. Kaylee gave him a huge hug informing him that he needed to visit. Aaron shook Chace's hand and thanked him for looking out for Hannah.

"I won't be far. I'll be able to hear when they announce the boarding process," Hannah informed her sister. Kaylee waved them off and turned back to the book she had been reading before they approached.

Chace led Hannah to a bench one gate down from hers so she would be able to hear the boarding call. He set his own carry-on bag down underneath the bench and took a seat. He had not been looking forward to this moment, and judging by Hannah's face he wasn't the only one.

Hannah sat silently beside him playing with the zipper on her jacket. He could see she was trying to hold back tears. He wrapped his arm around her and pulled her close. He would miss the feeling of her nearness.

"How often can I come to visit you?" he asked, breaking the silence. Hannah looked up at him and offered a smile.

"As often as you have time to spare," she replied giggling.

"Well, we are a little over six hours away from each other. It would make for short weekend visits, but I would gladly do it to be able to see you," he offered, taking her hand in his. Hannah sighed and leaned against him.

"You couldn't do that every weekend, Chace. That would be so much money," she frowned.

"Okay, how about we compromise. We'll each come to each other's place once a month for the weekend. So we would see each other two weekends out of the month. And on holiday weekends we would get an extra day," he explained.

"That sounds fair. I've never been to Tennessee before," she smiled. Making Hannah happy gave him pleasure. Seeing her smile up at him made his heart skip a beat.

"I really do mean it when I said that I want to make this relationship work. I know that we don't exactly live the closest, but where there's a will, there's a way. You mean a lot to me, Hannah," he declared, turning to face her.

"I can honestly say that I would have never let myself get into a long distance relationship before, but I have a very good feeling that this can be my exception. There's something about you that is different than any guy I have ever met, and I don't want to lose you," Hannah stated. Chace felt his heart soar hearing her sweet words.

Chace and Hannah reminisced about the fun times they had on the ship. He asked her about what she was planning on doing with the Hunter situation. She told him that she wasn't going to press charges and that she just wanted to leave it in the past. He wanted to see Hunter pay for what he did to her, but he knew she didn't want to go through all of that.

Chace soaked up each moment, each touch from Hannah. He knew the time was coming close that she needed to board her plane. The gate agent had already called a few times for passengers to start the boarding process. Sadness welled up within him as he heard her gate call for their last passengers.

~~*~*~*

"Last call for flight 3728 to Charlotte. Last call for flight 3728 to Charlotte," came the announcement Hannah had been dreading. She knew she needed to get going or she would risk missing her flight. Hannah pursed her lips and looked over to Chace. A look of melancholy flashed across his features and she could feel a tight ball forming in her throat.

"Let's get you to your gate," Chace suggested, standing and offering Hannah his hand. She stood and walked with him to where the final passengers for her flight were scurrying up turn in their tickets. He stopped her a few yards from the desk.

"Let me know when you get to Charlotte?" he asked softly. Hannah nodded, trying to keep her tears at bay.

"I'm going to miss you, Hannah. This past week has been the best week ever," he whispered, pulling her into a hug.

Don't cry yet! Don't cry yet! she chanted to herself.

"I'm going to miss you, too, Chace. I had so much fun being with you," she struggled to get the words out, her voice shaking at the end.

Chace took her face softly in his hands and brought her lips to his for one last heartfelt kiss. Hannah kissed him back earnestly and hugged him tight.

"Miss, are you on this flight?" asked the ticket agent. Hannah regretfully broke away from Chace's lips and nodded.

"I'm sorry, but I'll need you to board

now," the woman remarked woefully.

"I'll see you soon, beautiful," Chace voiced in her ear. A single tear escaped down Hannah's cheek at the sweetness in his voice.

"I'm looking forward to it," she tried to smile.

Sighing heavily, Hannah walked slowly to the ticket agent. The woman scanned her ticket and allowed her through. Each step felt like a hundred pounds as Hannah walked toward the plane. She knew she shouldn't have, but she glanced back to get one more glimpse of Chace. He stood there with a smile on his handsome face as he blew her a small kiss. Hannah smiled and blew a kiss right back to him before turning around the corner and entering the plane.

The flight attendant went through the routine explanation of safety instructions, but Hannah didn't hear a word. It was only when the plane began to back away from the terminal that she allowed her tears to flow.

February 13th, 2019

A couple of months passed by as Hannah got back into the swing of things after the cruise. The first few weeks had been difficult, not only for adjusting from her vacation, but from being unable to see Chace on a daily basis. But he kept to his word and they saw each other twice a month. They talked nightly on the phone, something Hannah looked forward to each day.

That weekend she was going out to Tennessee to visit. It was Valentines Day weekend and Chace had promised her a romantic weekend. Her shift at the bank she worked for ended at two o'clock and she was all ready to go once she got off.

"Any plans this weekend, Hannah?" asked her boss, Ryan. She poured herself a cup of water from the water cooler.

"Yes, I have plans with my boyfriend in Nashville," she replied, smiling happily.

"That's a far piece from here," Ryan stated, drinking his coffee. Hannah sighed, knowing all too well the truth of that statement.

"Yeah, I know. But he's worth it," she sighed dreamily. Ryan laughed softly.

"Well, since it's a special weekend for you, why don't you head out early," he suggested kindly. Hannah's eyes went wide, peeking over at the clock. It was only eleven.

"Are you sure? I've only been here for a few hours?" she questioned.

"Yeah, get on out of here. Drive safe. I expect to see you bright and early Monday morning," he demanded lightheartedly.

"Oh, thank you, Ryan! This is really kind of you," she expressed her gratitude excitedly.

Hannah clocked out saying a quick goodbye to her fellow tellers. She contemplated calling Chace, but decided not to. She wanted to surprise him. As she pulled out of the bank, her heart beat wildly with excitement. She couldn't wait to get to Tennessee.

~~*~*~*

Early that afternoon, Chace started to get his place ready for Hannah's arrival. He was more than happy to give his shift to a co-worker who needed to make up some hours. With it being Valentines Day weekend he wanted to make this a really special weekend for the two of them.

Chace decided he was going to tell Hannah that he loved her at their dinner the next night. He knew she wouldn't get in until that evening, but that gave him plenty of time to prepare.

Chace wanted to have a candle lit dinner for her with roses. Lots of roses. He looked around his kitchen to see what ingredients he needed to make for dinner the next night. With his list in hand, he headed for the store.

Scrolling up and down the aisles, Chace picked the items he needed. As he approached the produce section, he came to a sudden halt. There a few yards away from him looking at tomatoes was his ex, Lacy. He hadn't seen, or heard from, Lacy in years. He watched as she carefully examined each tomato to see which one she wanted.

Well, this is going to be awkward. I need tomatoes, he thought sighing.

Chace tried to avoid her by going to the lettuce first. He kept his back to her as he picked a bag of lettuce and moved on to the cucumbers. Glancing back, he saw that she was no longer in front of the tomatoes. Exhaling a quick breath, he pushed his cart over to the produce he needed.

"Oh my gosh! Chace, is that you?!" called a high pitched voice behind him.

Chace closed his eyes momentarily. He had failed in his attempt to bypass her. He turned around with an apprehensive smile on his face. Lacy stood there with her bag of tomatoes in one hand, her cell phone and pink puff ball key chain in the other.

"Lacy," he said, feeling unsettled by her sudden appearance. He turned his attention back to the tomatoes, but Lacy came around to his side.

"What are the odds!" she quipped, her white smile a contrast to her tan skin.

"It's been a while. How have you been?" she asked, trying to get his attention.

"Well, since you ask, I've been really good lately," he replied, thinking of Hannah.

"That's good! Hey, we should totally catch up! Why don't we have lunch or grab a cup of coffee?" Lacy prompted, her gum smacking her lips.

"I can't do that, Lacy. You've caught me shopping for a dinner I'm planning for my girlfriend," he responded.

It felt good to know he could be near her and not feel attracted to her anymore. Yes, she was still beautiful, but he didn't long for her. Inwardly he rejoiced at the fact that he was completely over her. Lacy, however, didn't look as ecstatic.

"Oh, new girlfriend, huh?" she asked, pretending to pout.

"What does it matter to you? You're the one who chose to be with another man while you were with me," Chace claimed, getting slightly annoyed. Lacy frowned shifting from one foot to the other.

"About that...I know I made a huge mistake, Chace. I should have never let myself get into that situation. That guy was a complete jerk," she grumbled, flipping her platinum blonde hair over her shoulder.

"Well, you did. I need to get going," said Chace, turning his cart to leave. The more he was around her the more annoying she became.

"Wait! Listen, I know I was wrong and I deserve for you not to want to speak to me, but I really am sorry. Please, just have coffee with me for old time's sake. We were really good together, Chace," begged Lacy, caressing his arm as he tried to pass her. His eyebrows pulled together in frustration.

"You had your chance. I gave you everything you ever wanted. I even moved to this stupid state for you! And all so you could cheat on me? No, it's not going to happen. Goodbye," he finalized, brushing her hand off of his and leaving her behind.

Flustered, Chace finally made it home. He set everything aside and went to relax on his couch. Looking at the clock on the wall he saw that it was five. Figuring that it would be another few hours before Hannah arrived, he decided to take a shower.

Chace felt better after his shower. His encounter with Lacy had put him in a bad mood. He couldn't believe she had asked for another chance. After what she did to him, he didn't care if he ever saw her again.

He wrapped the towel around his waist and went to his room to retrieve his clothes. As he walked over to his dresser he caught a glimpse of movement by the doorway. Quickly glancing over he was dumbfounded to see Lacy standing in the doorway of his room, smiling deviously at him.

"What the hell, Lacy?!" Chace shouted, gripping his towel firmly. Lacy laughed at his plight.

"I can't *believe* you didn't change the locks! Don't you remember I still had a key when I left?" she questioned slyly, waving the key in front of her.

"Well, it didn't occur to me that you would come back. You need to get out *now*," he demanded, pointing to the door.

"Oh come on, Chace! I saw the way you were acting in the store. I know you still have feelings for me," she insisted, walking over to him. She lightly swept her hand down his bare chest.

Is she crazy? he thought to himself as he recoiled from her touch.

"You are so full of yourself. I'm serious. Get out!" he yelled, making Lacy jump.

"I miss you, Chacey," she whined, using the nickname he use to think was cute. Now it sounded like nails on a chalk board.

"It's *over*, Lacy. There is no more us. I don't miss you and I have moved on. I'm happy and you need to accept that," he growled.

Before Lacy could respond Chace's doorbell rang. Stumped on who it could be, he walked the few steps to the window to peer outside. Panic engulfed him as he saw Hannah's car parked outside.

No, no, this can NOT be happening! his mind bellowed.

~~*~*~*

Hannah rang the doorbell a second time. She knew Chace was home because his car was parked in the driveway. A flashy silver mustang was parked in front of his house as well. Maybe he had a friend over. She *was* early and she didn't tell him she was coming this soon.

Hannah was about to ring the bell again when the doorknob twisted. Her heart raced at the thought of seeing Chace's surprised face. But as the door opened, she was greeted by a slender woman with blond, almost white, hair with a cheeky smile on her face.

"Well, hi there! You must be the girlfriend Chace told me about," the blond commented mischievously.

Hannah could hear someone running down the stairs. She looked past the woman to see Chace bounding down the last step in a towel, his hair wet. He stared at her, his eyes beseeching hers desperately.

"Hannah, it's not what you think!" he exclaimed, reaching out his hand. His other hand was holding tightly onto his towel.

Hannah's blood froze. She stood wide-eyed looking back and forth between the beautiful woman and Chace, and her heart began to crack. Confusion and betrayal played ping-pong in her mind as she tried to process what was going on.

"Don't look upset. He's all yours now," the blond stated brazenly as she walked past Hannah's motionless form on the porch. Hannah watched as she made her way to the mustang and drove off, a smirk on her cheeky face.

"Hannah, hear me out, please?" Chace begged. Hannah slowly turned her head back toward him. Tears of anger and heartache welled up in her eyes. He was shivering as a chilly February breeze blew.

"Please, come inside," he insisted, offering his hand out to her. Hannah looked at his hand and so badly wanted to take it, but pain pierced her so horribly that all she wanted to do was escape.

"I can't be here," she spoke, her voice wavering. Chace shook his head back and forth.

"No, Hannah, please don't go. Let me explain what happened," he urged her.

But Hannah stepped back from his hand and turned to jog hastily to her car. She turned the ignition forcefully and recklessly drove her car into the street and sped off not looking back.

Tears filled her eyes and blurred her vision. She knew she shouldn't be driving while she was crying like this. A few miles down the road, she saw a hotel and turned quickly into the parking lot. Not even bringing in her bag of clothing, Hannah walked up to the counter. A woman in her mid fifties turned around to greet her.

"Can I have a room, please?" Hannah inquired, wiping the tears from her face.

"Why of course you can, sugar plum. Is everythin' alright?" asked the heavyset woman, her southern accent thick.

"Yes, I just need a room," Hannah repeated as politely as she could. She could feel herself coming apart. The hotel receptionist gave her the key and Hannah paid for one night. She knew there was no way she could drive back home this late in the evening.

Hannah trudged her way to her room,

this time retrieving her bag, and plopped on the stiff hotel bed. The image of Chace in a towel would have been a pleasing memory, but was marred by the face of the mystery blond. Fresh tears streamed down her face.

Hannah's cell phone rang. She reached for the phone and hit ignore. Seeing she had ten missed calls and had three voice mails, all from Chace, she decided to listen to the messages.

"Hannah, please come back! You really need to know that what you're thinking isn't what happened. Nothing happened. If you'd just let me explain," his voice strained before the call dropped.

The next two messages were similar, but each call his voice became more and more emotional. It pulled at Hannah's heartstrings, but how was what she saw explainable for her benefit?

Nothing made sense. Hannah turned off her phone and tossed it on the floor. She couldn't deal with him right now. Feeling empty and alone, Hannah curled up on the bed and cried until she exhausted all her tears.

An hour later she woke up to a light knock at her hotel door. She had put up the do not disturb sign so she decided to ignore it. Another few knocks rapped on her door.

"Hannah, it's Lana! Please open up," Hannah heard Lana's muffled voice call to her. Perplexed, she pulled the blankets aside and peered out the curtain.

How on earth? she thought as she went to unlock the door. Lana's face was shocked as she took in the sight of her friend. Hannah was sure she looked awful.

"Can I come in?" Lana wanted to know. Hannah sniffled and moved aside so her friend could enter. Lana walked in and pulled Hannah into a hug.

"How did you know I was here?" Hannah asked, blowing her nose.

"Chace called Jake and told him what happened and said you might have gone to a hotel. He told us what your car looked like and Jake and I have been searching for you," she explained, sitting down on the bed with Hannah.

"Lana, I can't see him, if that's why you came here. It hurts too much to even talk about right now," she claimed, a few tears escaping down her freckled cheeks. Lana smiled gently and handed her another tissue.

"I'm not here to force you to do anything. But when Chace called us I could hear how upset he was over the whole situation. I figured maybe you would let *me* tell you what he said," Lana pursued cautiously.

Hannah sat for a moment contemplating whether or not she wanted to hear what Lana had to say. She trusted Lana and viewed her as a very close friend. But she had trusted Chace, too, and she wasn't sure if she could trust anyone right now.

"I'm sorry, Lana, but there couldn't possibly be a way for him to explain himself out of what I saw," she replied, looking down at the bed.

"He's not cheating on you, Hannah! Lacy showed up unexpectedly," Lana tried to explain.

That name alone was enough to cause a serious blow to Hannah's chest. She remembered Chace telling her about his ex and how she had cheated on him. She was the girlfriend he moved to Tennessee to be with.

"I'm not sure what to believe, and I mean no disrespect to you," Hannah stated. There was too much turmoil bubbling within her to have the right frame of mind to listen.

Lana looked at her with a sad expression. She shook her head and got up from the bed.

"I understand, but I *am* telling you the truth. Think about this, please," Lana insisted, walking out the door.

After hearing the soft click of the door, Hannah laid back down on the bed. She was too miserable to eat, even to the protest of her stomach. All she wanted to do was go home.

Early the next morning, Hannah collected her things and tossed them in the back seat of her car. Not even taking a shower, she drove off knowing the next six and a half hours would be agonizing.

February 16th, 2019

Chace tried relentlessly to reach Hannah over the weekend. The next morning he went to the hotel Lana told him she had gone to, but Hannah had already checked out. His heart sank lower and lower with each unanswered phone call.

An idea had been floating around that weekend in his mind that he needed to talk to Jake and Lana about. They were his closest friends and this idea involved them. Before calling them, he tried calling Hannah again.

"Hi, this is Hannah. Just leave me a message and I will get back to you," her cheery voicemail replied before beeping.

"Hey, Hannah, it's me. I just wanted to tell you that I've been thinking of you and I miss you. Please find it in your heart to call me.

I am only half of me without you," he said dejectedly. Reaching her voicemail was the only way he could hear her voice anymore.

Without any success reaching Hannah, he rang Jake.

"Hey, man, what's up?" Jake answered cheerfully.

Jake and Lana had been trying to cheer him up all weekend. Jake had to drag him to work that morning. Even then Chace had struggled to make it through the work day.

"Hey, Jake. I was wondering if I could talk with you and Lana about something important," Chace prompted.

"Yeah, that'd be fine. How about we meet up for dinner tonight?" Jake offered.

"Okay, that'll work," he replied.

"Awesome. Why don't we meet at six o'clock at Red Line Bar & Grill?" Jake suggested.

"I'll meet you guys there," said Chace, hanging up.

It was four-thirty when he got off the phone with Jake. Knowing that he was really going to try and go through with his plan, he decided that he should pay a visit to his bank. There were a few things he needed to get in order before meeting up with his friends.

Later that evening, Chace arrived at the restaurant and made his way to where Jake and Lana were sitting. Lana got up and gave him a hug.

"I am so happy you came out tonight!" she exclaimed.

"I'm glad you guys agreed to come,"

Chace smiled.

"Hello! My name is Vicky. Is there something I can get you started on to drink?" asked the waitress kindly. Chace told her what beer he wanted and she was off in a flash.

"So what's this all about?" asked Jake, taking a drink of his beer.

Chace inhaled slowly. Before he began, the waitress set his beer down and the group ordered what they wanted for dinner. She took all the menus and disappeared once again.

"Okay, so I have a plan in mind that you guys will probably think I'm crazy for wanting to do," Chace started, turning his beer slowly in circles. He was nervous to propose such an idea. He was also anxious because if they declined his offer he wouldn't be able to go through with his plan.

"Well, spill it. I'm sure we've heard crazier," laughed Lana.

"Alright, well, I've made up my mind that I am going to be moving back to North Carolina," he stated, gauging the looks on his friends' faces. Jake's face registered surprise, and Lana's expression told him she knew why. She narrowed her eyes with a smile.

"Hannah, right?" she inquired smugly. Chace nodded, reaching for his beer.

"That's a big move, but not very crazy," Jake chuckled.

"No, that's not the crazy part. The crazy part is that I want to move by the end of next week," he said, dropping the bomb. Both Jake and Lana fixed their wide-eyed gazes on him.

"Are you serious?" questioned Lana.

"Very. I can't stand being away from Hannah anymore. Plus, you know I've been wanting to move back to North Carolina," Chace mentioned.

Vicky returned to their table with their food on a tray. She disbursed the food to each of them with a smile, and asked if there was anything else they needed. All three answered with a no and she left to tend to her next table.

"Chace, what about your house? You can't possibly sell it that quickly," Jake commented as he took a bite of his food.

"Well, I knew you would ask. That is the reason I wanted to meet up with you guys. I went to the bank earlier. I talked to them about my options for selling my house under the situations I've proposed. They gave me a few ideas, one of which I'm highly in favor of, but it is asking a lot of you guys," Chace started off. Lana and Jake exchanged puzzled looks with each other before turning back to Chace.

"How does it involve us?" Lana asked curiously.

Here goes nothing... Chace thought, bracing himself for their response to his proposition.

"The bank told me one of the ways I could go through with my plan is to set someone up as power of attorney over the sale of my house," he answered, sending up a silent prayer.

"I've heard of that, actually. You want *us* to take that position?" asked Jake, his fork paused in midair.

"I know it's a lot to ask of you guys, but it would ensure the sale of my house without filing for a deed in lieu of foreclosure. If I do that it will reflect negatively on my credit, along with foreclosing or doing a short sale," said Chace, breaking down the information.

"Do you mind if we take a night to consider this?" questioned Lana.

"Yeah, of course. I wasn't expecting you guys to answer right away," he replied.

"Honestly, I don't think it would be a problem. I just want to go over what all is involved in the process," Lana stated, looking over at her husband.

"You know me. I would have said yes already without thinking, but that's why I married her," Jake laughed, nudging Lana. Chace smiled at his friends.

"It is a good thing you married her, for multiple reasons. Someone has to be the brain," Chace joked. Lana rolled her eyes.

"I am on board, Chace. You know I am. I'd just like to do my research before committing to something like this," she smiled innocently. Chace understood. He knew he was asking a huge favor of them.

After the group finished their dinner, they went their separate ways. Lana promised Chace that she would have an answer for him that night or the next morning. He hoped that it would be the latter of the two. He felt suspended in time as he waited as patiently as he could for his friends phone call.

Later that night, Chace got the call from Jake and Lana confirming that they would go ahead with being a power of attorney over the sale of his home. He was so excited, and more than anything he wanted to call Hannah. But he didn't know how she would take the news, or if she even checked his messages.

Deciding it was time to get some ducks in a row, Chace made a phone call to his parents. He knew they would be over the moon excited for him to move back. They had been begging him to come home for years.

"Hello?" answered the familiar female voice on the other line.

"Hey, Mom. I have some news for you," Chace announced as he went into detail about his plans.

February 28th, 2019

"Hannah, do you think I should find out the gender of my baby? Or should I wait and be surprised?" asked Kaylee from Hannah's living room.

Kaylee was hanging out at Hannah's house that Saturday afternoon. The two had plans to catch a movie in the evening since Aaron was working. Kaylee had been at Hannah's frequently since her unexpected return from Tennessee weeks back. She had started to worry when Hannah slipped into a slight depression.

Hannah walked into the living room from the kitchen with two glasses of water.

"Well, I, for one, want to know the moment the doctors are able to find out," she replied, sitting on her comfy chair across from

Kaylee.

"See, I want to know, too, but something about the suspense of waiting is alluring as well. Aaron wants to find out ASAP. He thinks it's going to be a boy," she chuckled, tucking her feet underneath her legs.

"If you wait until the last minute how will you decorate? How will anyone know what to get you? And personally I think the baby is a girl," declared Hannah smiling.

"Alright, I won't wait. I probably wouldn't be able to anyway," Kaylee surrendered.

Hannah felt her phone vibrate in her pocket. Pulling it out she saw Chace's name flash across her screen. There used to be a picture, but it hurt too much to see his face as frequently as he called. Chace's calls didn't go unnoticed by Hannah. She never answered, but she listened to each voicemail, shedding a few tears for each message.

"Is that him?" Kaylee inquired. Hannah set the phone down on the table by her drink, nodding to her sister.

"Hannah, when are you going to answer him? He has called you every day since you got back and you haven't answered once. Don't you think he deserves to at least get his side of the story out to you?" Kaylee wanted to know.

It had taken all of Hannah's strength *not* to answer Chace's phone calls and text messages. But she just couldn't see how there was any other explanation for what she had witnessed. And even if she did hear him out, could she believe him?

"I can't, Kaylee. I want to, but I just can't. I saw what I saw and there is nothing he can say to make it different," she answered.

"But what if there is another side to it? You could be throwing away a once in a lifetime relationship," Kaylee remarked, sadness filling her voice.

"Kaylee, he was pretty much naked and she was in the house with him! His ex! What else could have possibly been going on?" Hannah questioned her sister.

"I know it seems bad, but I honestly believe there's another side. Innocent until proven guilty," said Kaylee, trying to reason with her. Hannah shook her head.

"I believe having another woman, especially that woman, answer the door and having him running down the stairs in a towel is a guilty verdict for me," she commented, tears blurring her vision. Kaylee got up and pulled her sister into a hug.

"I know it's hard. Just hang in there, okay? Everything will work out as it is supposed to," she soothed. Hannah sighed into their embrace and glanced over at her wall clock.

"I had better go grab a few things from the store to make for dinner tonight," she mentioned, pulling away from her sister and wiping her eyes.

"You know we can just go out to eat," Kaylee offered as Hannah went for her purse.

"Yeah, but I've eaten out a lot lately because I haven't wanted to cook. I need to get out of that habit. Do you want to come with me?" she asked.

"No, I'm going to stay here and rest. I feel constantly drained anymore," replied Kaylee, laying down on the couch.

"You know you can use the bed in the spare room," Hannah suggested.

"Nah, your couch is very comfortable. Besides, I don't want to be out for too long," Kaylee laughed.

Hannah smiled at her sister. She couldn't imagine what it would be like to have a child developing inside of her. With all the changes happening in a pregnant woman's body, Hannah wasn't surprised that Kaylee was tired all the time.

All her life Hannah had wanted to experience the joy of bringing a child into the world with the man she loved. But those dreams seemed more distant than ever after what happened with Chace. She didn't even want to think about dating, marriage or love because it all brought pain to her heart. And Hannah didn't want to date another man. She only wanted Chace.

~~*~*~*

Chace had spent the previous day driving a U-Haul with all his belongings while his dad drove behind in Chace's car. His mother followed in her car. Arriving in Raleigh late that evening, Chace was spent. He knew he wouldn't be able to drive to Charlotte until morning. His parents had offered to let him keep the U-Haul at their house while he made his drive to Hannah's.

By mid morning the next day, Chace made his trek to Charlotte, his stomach full of jitters. He knew he was taking a serious risk not knowing if Hannah would even see him, but he had to try. She just had to let him explain what happened that horrible day.

Arriving in Charlotte a little after three o'clock, Chace made his way to Hannah's street.

When he pulled up in front of her house, Hannah's car wasn't in the driveway. Chace's spirits dropped. How would he know when she was going to be home? He sat in his car for a few minutes deliberating what he should do. Looking back at the house he saw someone walk in front of the front window. He immediately recognized Kaylee's fiery red hair.

On a whim, Chace turned off his car and walked up to the front door. Not knowing whether or not Kaylee would be friendly toward him made Chace uneasy, but he pushed on, ringing the doorbell. After a moment the door creaked open and Kaylee stood in the doorway, an awestruck expression plastered on her freckled face.

"Hey," he greeted.

"Now *this* is a surprise," Kaylee commented, crossing her arms in front of her chest. Chace couldn't tell if she was happy or upset with him.

"Um, is Hannah home by chance?" he asked, clearing his throat.

"She went out to the store," Kaylee answered. Chace didn't know what to say. He didn't feel that he could invite himself in.

"You have a lot of nerve showing your

face here," Kaylee chastised him. Chace looked her in the eye.

"I know you might think that, but I *need* Hannah to let me tell her the truth about what happened," his voice pleaded.

Kaylee uncrossed her arms and moved out of the doorway. Sweeping out her arm, she motioned for Chace to enter. Surprised, he nodded his head to her and walked in.

"Thank you. But why did you let me in if you think I'm guilty?" Chace asked confused. Kaylee sat down on the couch and motioned for him to sit down across from her.

"I'm not the one casting the guilty verdict. *Yet*," she stated, eyeing him carefully. Chace blew out a breath and began to tell her what happened that awful day. She sat patiently and allowed him to finish before she spoke.

"To be honest, I believe you. I really do. I didn't really think you would do something like that, just from how I've seen you treat my sister. But *she* is the one who you'll be hard pressed to convince," she stated pointedly.

"I know. She won't return my calls or my messages," he said, his shoulders drooping.

"Hannah still cares a lot about you. She has been in pretty bad shape these past few weeks," she informed him. Chace winced thinking about the torture her thoughts must have been putting her through.

"Do you think she would be mad if she came home and I was here?" he asked Kaylee.

"I'm not sure how she would react. But I think it's time she heard you out," she responded, nodding her head toward the front window. Chace's heart raced as he saw Hannah's car pulling up to the house. He watched her walk up the sidewalk to the door.

"Kaylee, they didn't have the dark chocolate candy you wanted me to get," Hannah called as she closed the door behind her.

Her attention was directed to the multiple bags she was trying to carry in all at once. Chace stood up as she entered. When she turned around she abruptly dropped all of the bags dumbfounded.

"Chace!" she gasped.

~~*~*~*

Hannah felt dizzy. She looked back and forth between Chace and Kaylee in confusion. Why was he here? Did Kaylee have something to do with this? Questions spun around in her head like a hurricane.

"Why are you here?" Hannah asked, directing her question at Chace. He stayed where he was but pleaded to her with his eyes.

"I came because we need to talk, Hannah," he answered.

"Did you know he was coming?" she asked her sister. Kaylee stood up from the couch and came over to her side.

"No, I didn't. But I do agree that you need to talk with him," Kaylee answered firmly.

Feeling panicked, Hannah dropped down and grabbed as many bags as she could and rushed past her sister to the kitchen. She heard footsteps behind her and turned to see Chace following her.

On one hand it felt so good to see him. After not talking to him for a couple of weeks, seeing him made her insides bubble. His handsome face had a slight amount of stubble growing on his chin and under his nose. If anything, that made him look even more attractive.

But the other part of her wanted to scream at him for showing up at her door. She was still so undecided on how she felt, and seeing him didn't help. Old memories dredged up of him in a towel as Lacy answered the door to his house, leaving a bitter taste in her mouth.

Hannah busied herself with putting the groceries away. Chace stood quietly out of her way for a moment, but soon stepped up to her. He took the items in her hand and placed them on the counter.

"Hannah, please talk to me," he spoke softly. She shivered at the smooth tone of his voice. How she had missed him. She looked down at the floor, unable to look him in the eye.

"There is nothing to talk about, Chace. You did the unthinkable," Hannah murmured, resentfulness coloring her words.

"And just what is it that you think I did?" he challenged. Hannah shot him a look of indignation at his question. Did he think her so naive?

"You were in a towel when Lacy, *your ex Lacy,* answered *your* door, Chace! If there was nothing to hide, why were you racing down the stairs? She seemed just fine letting me in on the show," Hannah spat as she walked briskly past him back into the living room. All the anger and hurt that had been bottling up within her was now coming to the surface.

"Would you just listen to me?" Chace demanded, his voice escalating.

"Hannah, stop. You can't keep running from this," said Kaylee, putting her hands out to halt her sister.

By now tears were flowing generously down Hannah's face. She felt like she was beginning to come apart. Stopped in front of her sister, she begged her silently to let her go. Kaylee shook her head.

"You need to deal with this now," Kaylee spoke softly before stepping off into the spare bedroom.

The door clicked softly and Hannah slowly turned to face Chace. He gradually approached her until he was a foot in front of her. Without saying a word he pulled her into a hug. All of Hannah's tears were released as he held her tightly in his arms. It felt so good to be in his embrace again. She wanted to stay like that forever.

"Why? Why did you cheat on me?" she cried, resting her forehead on his chest.

"Hannah, why would I cheat on you if I love you?" he asked in a hushed voice. Hannah's eyes flew open as she pulled back from his hold.

"What did you say?" she inquired, hoping her mind wasn't playing tricks on her. Chace smiled and pulled her over to the couch with him.

"I love you, Hannah Lane," he announced, holding her hands.

Hannah's breath caught in her throat. She had dreamed of him saying those three words to her.

But how can he love me after what he did? she thought to herself. A little voice inside of her told her to listen to what he had to say.

"How can you expect me to believe that?" she whispered, tears clinging to her eyelashes.

"Because I didn't cheat on you. Lacy saw me at the store while I was getting ingredients for a special dinner I was going to make you on Valentines Day. She asked me to have coffee with her and I told her I was dating someone. I went home and I took a shower because you weren't supposed to be arriving until later that evening.

"When I got out of the shower Lacy was standing in the doorway of my bedroom, waving *her* key to *my* house in front of me. She asked why I never changed the locks and I told her I never expected her to come back. It had been years since Lacy and I had any contact, so why would I have thought she would keep a key, let alone use it?

"So anyway, she tried to come on to me, but I wouldn't let her. And at that time, you had just pulled up and were at my doorstep. Lacy got to the door before me and did what she does best. She deceived you into thinking something might have been going on. But nothing was going on, Hannah. What I just told you is exactly how it happened," Chace finalized.

Hannah took a moment to let what he had told her sink in. Could it be true? Something *that* off the wall? She looked over at him and she could see no deception. Looking into his eyes was like looking into his soul. His honest soul. He really hadn't been cheating on her.

Chace leaned over and tucked his finger underneath her chin. He brought her gaze level with his. She could see the love flowing from his eyes.

"I love you, Hannah!" he proclaimed, stroking her chin softly with his thumb. Tears welled up in Hannah's eyes as a smile crept onto her face.

"I love you, Chace!"

~Epilogue~

May 20th, 2019

It was a bright, beautiful day. Perfect weather for moving day. Jake and Lana were able to successfully sell Chace's home the previous month and he was able to find a house in Charlotte close to his new job, and to Hannah.

He had taken Hannah to meet his family in Raleigh and she instantly loved them. They had let Chace use their storage unit to hold his belongings until he was able to find a place to stay. He had been living at Hannah's house in her spare bedroom.

It had been an amazing few months spent with him. Hannah fell more and more in love with him as they continued to get to know each other, and grow in their relationship. Everything seemed to be working out and she couldn't have been happier.

"Where do you want these boxes?" Jake

asked Chace, bringing in three large boxes on his dolly. Jake and Lana had driven out to help him move and to celebrate. They were staying at Hannah's place since Chace was moving into his.

"Those are marked bedroom, so down the hall, last room on the right," Chace instructed.

Kaylee and Aaron had also joined the party and Kaylee came out of the kitchen with fresh lemonade. She was not allowed to help with the move since she was almost six months pregnant. Everyone stopped to take a break from their hard work.

"I think we're almost done," said Aaron, taking a big gulp the lemonade. Jake nodded.

"Yeah, we only have about six more boxes to go and then the U-Haul will be empty," he stated.

"Awesome! Aaron and I can take the truck back to U-Haul," Kaylee offered, caressing the small mound on her stomach.

"That will work. I'll give you guys some cash to fill it up before you return it," said Chace, reaching into his wallet, giving Aaron the money.

"We'll catch you guys later," waved Kaylee as she followed Aaron out the door.

"Do you guys want some help setting up any furniture?" asked Lana.

"Nah, I think Hannah and I can handle it. You guys have helped out so much already. I really can't thank you enough for helping me sell my house in Tennessee. I wouldn't have been able to do this without you," he thanked the couple. Jake and Lana smiled.

"We were happy to help and glad that everything went smoothly," Lana replied.

"Do you guys want to follow me back to my house so you can relax?" Hannah asked.

"No, that's okay. We can plug your address into our GPS and get ourselves there," Jake answered.

"Okay. The spare key is under the welcome mat. Feel free to help yourself to anything," she smiled as the couple stood up to leave.

"See you later," they said simultaneously.

Hannah and Chace worked side by side throughout the afternoon and into the early evening. Together they had successfully assembled Chace's bed, placed furniture throughout the house, and unpack some of his belongings. Hannah had worked in the kitchen putting dishes and food away while Chace unpacked his clothes and set up his room.

"I don't know about you, but I am starving," Chace commented, coming into the kitchen. Hannah was finishing up as she separated the silverware into the correct slots.

"I could go for some food," she agreed, closing the drawer.

"I was looking on my phone and found a nice place I want to take you to," he mentioned, walking over to Hannah and wrapping her up in his arms. She smiled and looked into the eyes of the man she loved. She still couldn't believe he was there.

"And where's that?" she inquired curiously.

"Stagioni. They have outdoor patio

seating and I made a reservation," Chace replied. Hannah knew about the restaurant, but had never been there.

"Do I have time to shower? I'm kind of dirty from all the moving," she commented, looking down at her clothing.

"Well, you always look good to me, but yes, our reservation is in an hour. I should probably wash up, too. I can pick you up in about forty-five minutes," he suggested.

"That should be good. I should get going then," she declared, picking up her keys.

"Not just yet," he said, as he lifted her up and set her on the counter in front of him.

Hannah squealed joyously and wrapped her arms around his neck. Chace pulled her close to the edge of the counter until they were inches apart. She smiled playing with the hair at the nape of his neck. He looked into her eyes with such intensity that she thought she would melt into a puddle.

"I love you, Hannah," he whispered, his voice raspy. Hannah felt her skin tingle.

"I love you, too, Chace," she replied softly.

He wrapped his arms around her and leaned in to kiss her. Hannah sighed into the kiss. She felt his love pour into his kiss, and her heart fluttered with happiness. Never had she felt such passion for someone.

An hour later, Chace walked Hannah into the restaurant and gave the hostess his name for the reservation. She smiled politely and led them to a table for two on the back patio. A light breeze blew Hannah's hair around, and the temperature couldn't be better.

"You look beautiful," Chace complimented.

"Thank you. I've wanted to wear this outfit purely to go with my necklace," she giggled, holding up the turquoise necklace he had given her on the cruise. He grinned as he pulled out the mermaid tail necklace she had given him that same night.

They ordered their dinner and Chace requested a special bottle of wine. The waiter smiled agreeably and went off. Hannah felt like a princess the way he was treating her. The small table was lit by two candles twinkling with each soft breeze that blew, and a white rose sat in a vase in between the candles.

"Chace, you didn't have to do that," she murmured.

"Oh, but I do," he responded, wiggling his eyebrows up and down. Hannah laughed.

"How did I get so lucky to have you?" she asked, offering a playful smirk.

"Well, that's easy. You're an angel. The real question is how did *I* get so lucky? That cruise was the best vacation I have ever taken. I still can't believe that's how we met," he said astonishingly.

"It's crazy, right? Of all the places to meet someone I would have never guessed it would have been there. But here we are months down the road," she smiled.

Chace adjusted himself in his chair and ran his fingers through his hair. Hannah thought he looked worked up for some reason. He sucked in a deep breath, his hands folded in front of his lips, elbows propped on the table.

His eyes closed momentarily before he blew out his pent up breath in a whoosh.

Why is he acting so strange? she thought to herself curiously.

When he opened his eyes again, Hannah saw determination register on his face. He reached out for her hands, each on one side of the table. She rested her hands in his and smiled at him, puzzled.

"Hannah, meeting you on that cruise was the best thing that has ever happened to me. You mean so much to me and I am so in love with you. I've never met anyone like you before. Someone who makes me want to be a better person. Someone who is my better half," he spoke sincerely to her.

Hannah smiled lovingly at his words. She was about to respond, but Chace stood up and reached into his pocket. Kneeling down on one knee beside her, he looked up at her nervously as her eyes went wide with shock.

"Hannah Lane, will you marry me?" he purposed, opening the black velvet box.

A square solitaire diamond ring sat snugly inside the velvet slot sparkling up at her. Hannah's hands flew to her mouth as she looked down at Chace on his knee. He gazed up at her with a hopeful expression on his face.

"Yes," she replied softly, tears of happiness stinging her eyes.

Chace beamed as he took the ring out of the box and placed it on Hannah's left ring finger before jumping up and twirling her around. She laughed freely in his arms as he set her down.

A few yards away Hannah heard clapping and hollering. She looked behind her as Kaylee, Aaron, Jake and Lana came bounding toward them. Hannah's mouth fell open when she saw Jake holding a camera. She turned back to see Chace wink at her.

"Congratulations, you guys!" Lana gushed, hugging Hannah tightly.

"Thank you," she sniffled, wiping her tears aside. Chace walked over to her side as Kaylee stood in front of her.

"I told you," she smiled smugly. Hannah looked at her stumped.

"Told me what?" she inquired. Kaylee laughed.

"On the cruise the first day you met Chace. I told you that you were going to marry him," Kaylee stated, pulling her sister into a hug. Hannah remembered her sister telling her that and she giggled within the hug.

"I'm so happy for you," Kaylee whispered.

"Thank you, Kaylee!" Hannah commented.

Chace tapped her on the shoulder and passed her a glass of wine. She hadn't even realized the waiter had brought it out. Everyone raised their glasses, Kaylee's a glass of water, as Jake made a toast.

"To an amazing couple who deserve to be together. May your marriage be filled with love, trust, honesty and happiness. To Chace and Hannah!" he announced.

"To Chace and Hannah," everyone repeated before clinking their glasses together.

Hannah's heart was soaring as Chace

came over and kissed her sweetly. She couldn't imagine a more perfect moment.

"My bounty is as boundless as the sea, My love as deep; the more I give to thee, The more I have, for both are infinite," Chace quoted from Shakespeare's Romeo and Juliet. Hannah smiled up at her husband-to-be, a Shakespearian quote of her own up her sleeve.

"I know no ways to mince it in love, but directly to say, I love you."

CPSIA information can be obtained
at www.ICGtesting.com
Printed in the USA
BVHW071920080919
557876BV00001B/100/P